Vows of Silence

Storybook written by

Gail Hamilton

Based on the Sullivan Films Production
written by Gail Hamilton
adapted from the novels of

Lucy Maud Montgomery

A BANTAM SKYLARK BOOK®
NEW YORK · TORONTO · LONDON · SYDNEY · AUCKLAND

Based on the Sullivan Films Production produced by Sullivan Films Inc. in association with CBC and the Disney Channel with the participation of Telefilm Canada adapted from Lucy Maud Montgomery's novels.

Teleplay written by Gail Hamilton
Copyright © 1991 by Sullivan Films Distribution, Inc.

This edition contains the complete text
of the original edition.
NOT ONE WORD HAS BEEN OMITTED.

RL 6, 008–012

VOWS OF SILENCE
A Bantam Skylark Book / published by arrangement with
HarperCollins Publishers Ltd.

PUBLISHING HISTORY
HarperCollins edition published 1995
Bantam edition / March 1995

ROAD TO AVONLEA is the trademark of Sullivan Films Inc.

Skylark Books is a registered trademark of Bantam Books,
a division of Bantam Doubleday Dell Publishing Group, Inc.
Registered in U.S. Patent and Trademark Office and elsewhere.

ISBN 0-553-48126-6

Bantam Books are published by Bantam Books, a division of Bantam Doubleday Dell
Publishing Group, Inc. Its trademark, consisting of the words "Bantam Books" and the
portrayal of a rooster, is Registered in U.S. Patent and Trademark Office and in other
countries. Marca Registrada. Bantam Books, 1540 Broadway, New York, New York 10036.

PRINTED IN THE UNITED STATES OF AMERICA
OPM 0 9 8 7 6 5 4 3 2 1

Chapter One

The people of Avonlea were generally a church-going lot. After all, church services were more than just religious occasions. They were also social gatherings—a chance to see your neighbor's new hat, or to notice which young ladies blushed when certain young men caught their eye over the hymn-books. For many church members, the pews also provided a handy place to have a snooze while the minister droned on.

On one particular Sunday, the Avonlea Presbyterian Church was fuller than usual. In fact, it was packed to the seams. The increased attendance was due, not to any outbreak of religious enthusiasm, but to avid curiosity. The church had a new minister, and everyone was keen to hear him speak. After all, he was bound to be the main subject of conversation at Lawson's general store for the rest of the week!

Before they could get to the sermon, though, the congregation had to work its way through the required number of announcements, prayers and hymns. To this end, they plunged stoutly into the last verse of hymn number 424, "The Contrite Heart." They were ably accompanied by Mrs. Rachel Lynde, who pumped the church organ with her usual vigorous efficiency.

> There is a holy sacrifice
> Which God in heaven will not despise;
> Nay which is precious in His Eyes
> The Contrite Heart.

Even Mrs. Lynde was startled by the loudness behind her. The singing, she found, was being led by a fresh voice, strong and resonant, that boomed from the front of the church. The voice belonged to the new minister himself, the Reverend Hugh Fitzsimmons. When the hymn ended, the good Reverend held onto the last note far longer than anyone else.

Quite oblivious to all the surprised stares, he kept his eyes screwed shut in holy fervor as every other sound around him died away. Here was a man who either loved to sing—or just loved the sound of his own voice, no matter what it was doing.

Alec King, in a front pew with his family, gave his wife a poke as they sat down. "Our new pastor thinks he's Caruso," he whispered under his breath to Janet, who had to stifle a giggle at the thought that their new minister might be compared to the foremost operatic tenor of the day.

As everyone got settled, Felix King, who had been out seeing to the horse, scurried back to where his family was sitting—all except baby Daniel, his little brother, who wasn't yet a year old and had no interest whatever in new ministers.

Felix was eleven years old, and just at the age when boys are considered to be at their most obnoxious, especially by their older sisters. Felicity, who was all of fourteen, quite often thought her brother the most irritating creature on the planet—and Felix, brimful of mischief, did his best to live up to her opinion. Squeezing into the pew, Felix deliberately jostled his sister. His mother, who had eyes in the back of her head, saw what was happening and swiftly intervened to prevent open warfare. Felix grinned infuriatingly and sat down beside ten-year-old Cecily, well out of range of Felicity's pinching fingers.

Olivia Dale, the younger of Alec's two sisters, leaned towards her older sister, Hetty.

"Well, he certainly can sing, surely," said Olivia.

Olivia had a generous nature and tended to uncritical appreciation of anything that pleased her. Hetty, on the other hand, was the Avonlea schoolteacher and a hardened veteran of dozens of school musicals. She wasn't about to be carried away by fancy vocalizing.

"But can he preach?" asked Hetty.

Somehow, Olivia knew that her sister was very soon going to have a firm opinion on that subject.

Reverend Fitzsimmons stepped into the pulpit. He fussed with his notes for a moment, all the time smiling pleasantly and nodding vaguely at the congregation. Despite his small, round glasses and balding head, the minister was very young. He was also very pink in the face with the excitement of addressing his first real congregation. His collar had obviously been painstakingly starched in preparation for the big day.

The people of the village settled in as he prepared to speak. This promised to be an entertainment event of major proportions. Everyone waited eagerly for the new minister to strut his stuff.

"I'm hoping the large turnout today is not only curiosity as to how well the new pastor preaches," Fitzsimmons began conversationally, much as though he were chatting in a parlor. His small spectacles twinkled as he spoke.

Hetty King, a real stickler for proprieties, frowned at this informal style even as Olivia nudged her.

The preacher leaned forward, perusing the faces before him. As he did so, the pulpit groaned and tilted under his weight, almost throwing him off his feet. Rachel Lynde, who headed the pulpit committee, jumped up in embarrassment.

"I have been assured that the new pulpit will arrive here a week Wednesday, Reverend Fitzsimmons," she assured him hurriedly.

The committee had hoped to have the pulpit in place earlier, but it was impossible to hurry Hank Webster when he mixed up plain carpentry with producing a work of art.

Fitzsimmons nodded mildly and righted himself.

"It's a poor workman who blames his tools— though a sturdy pulpit means a sturdy church."

While the congregation worked that one out, he paused and shuffled his notes again.

"Well, let's get to my sermon, then." He surveyed the congregation again thoughtfully. "My colleagues in Toronto congratulated me on my posting in Avonlea. They said the sins here on this calm island must be small, inconsequential. Do you know what I told them?"

The people were already smiling a little in anticipation of hearing their superior virtues praised by this admiring outsider. As the silence stretched out, their smiles became puzzled. Reverend Fitzsimmons was pausing so long that the congregation began to think he actually expected an answer to his question. Hank Webster, in the front pew, was preparing to speculate aloud when Fitzsimmons suddenly let out a bellow.

"THERE ARE NO SUCH THINGS AS SMALL SINS! ASK LOT'S WIFE, TURNED TO A PILLAR OF SALT SIMPLY FOR LOOKING OVER HER SHOULDER!"

Simultaneously, Fitzsimmons smashed his fist down on the decrepit pulpit, causing a piece of it to break off under his blow and crash to the floor. The entire congregation was as startled as if someone had set off a bomb in their midst. Bert Potts, slumbering peacefully beside his wife, Clara, jerked bolt upright. Rachel Lynde seized her heart. Hetty King nearly lost her hat as her head shot up. And, mindful of Lot's wife, not a single person dared turn and look behind.

"That man's voice could cut steel!" Alec muttered to his wife as he tried to regain his composure.

"Not to mention what it could do to solid oak," Janet whispered back, looking at the mutilated pulpit.

Without apparently noticing the piece of oak spinning on the floor, or his gape-mouthed audience, Reverend Fitzsimmons went roaring on.

"SINS ARE LIKE THE PIRANHA FISH OF THE AMAZON! THEY GATHER AND MULTIPLY UNTIL THE MUDDY WATER BOILS WITH THEIR PERFIDY AND THE POOR SINNER'S FLESH IS RIPPED AND TORN UNTIL NOTHING BUT POLISHED WHITE BONE REMAINS."

More of the same followed. Much more. The harmless-looking Reverend turned out to have such a store of terrifying ammunition in his scriptural arsenal that the congregation left the church white-faced and shell-shocked. It took several large gulps of bracing Island air to restore them. As buggies hurriedly rolled away and families set out on foot from the church door, it was clear they could hardly wait to get home and discuss the event over the familiar comfort of their Sunday dinner.

Chapter Two

That evening, as was the Sunday custom of the King family, they all gathered at the farmhouse for a grand family meal. Hetty had come over from Rose Cottage, where she lived with her niece, Sara Stanley. Olivia Dale was there, leaving her retiring husband, Jasper, at home. The adults sat around the big main dining table while the young people had a table all their own nearby. Cecily, Felicity and Felix shared it with Sara, who, though nearly thirteen, was still child enough to be impatient with Felicity's grown-up airs.

While everyone was occupied with their roast beef, Felix took the opportunity to slip a bone from his plate to Digger, the family dog, who had positioned himself hopefully at Felix's feet. It was strictly forbidden to feed the dog from the table, and Felicity, ever on the watch, caught Felix in the act.

"Felix, don't feed the dog under the table," she snapped, leaping on him immediately.

"It's just a bone, Felicity."

Felix slipped a second tidbit to Digger, just to annoy his sister, and grinned.

At the larger table, Alec and Janet sat amid the good china with Hetty and Olivia. They were finishing up with the main course and speeding on to the hottest topic of conversation in the village.

"Apparently, the new minister's luggage included a box that was three times the size of a steamer trunk," Olivia was telling everyone, "and weighed absolutely nothing." Naturally, everything the Reverend Fitzsimmons brought with him had to be noticed and commented upon in such a small community.

"What could that be?" Janet wondered, passing around the potatoes.

Hetty tipped a napkin to her lips. She wore her hair severely scraped back into a bun, throwing her ears into rather unfortunate prominence. She didn't stand for fuss or nonsense from anyone, not even ministers bent on her personal salvation.

"Kites," she revealed in a rather scandalized tones. "Elvira Lawson told me. It seems the Reverend Fitzsimmons likes to fly kites."

Eyebrows popped up all around the table. In Avonlea, nobody over the age of ten played with kites.

"He does seem an odd sort," Janet observed, unable to forget how much she had been rattled by the sermon. She hoped all her future Sundays weren't going to be unrelieved salvos of fire and brimstone from the pulpit.

Alec felt compelled to come to the minister's defense. It wasn't right to work the fellow over after only one Sunday sermon.

"I'm sure he'll work out fine."

"He confuses piety with loudness," snorted Janet, the hellfire thundering still ringing in her ears.

"Reverend Fitzsimmons is young and perhaps a little overenthusiastic," Alec returned, not wanting to publicly disagree with his wife but determined to be fair.

Felix, his back to his father, rolled his eyes and contorted his face in comic imitation of Reverend Fitzsimmons. "He bellows like a steer," he snickered, looking as steer-like as he possibly could without getting caught by the adults. When they turned around and saw him anyway, he wiped his expression clean. "What'd I say?" he demanded innocently.

"Do you think you could behave yourself when your aunts are here, Felix dear?" Janet requested sweetly, not forgetting that Hetty was also the schoolmistress. Janet was a King by marriage, and sometimes she felt the critical eyes of Alec's relatives glaring upon herself and the behavior of her children.

"And occasionally," Alec added wryly, "when they're not?"

"That's why I don't want Felix around during our meeting," Felicity grumbled. "He *blurts* things."

"What meeting?" Alec wanted to know.

"Oh ... yes, Alec." Janet leaned towards her husband. "While you were visiting your brother Roger in Halifax, Felicity arranged a discussion group called the, uh, the Colicky Something-or-other ..."

"The Avonlea Young Women's Colloquium for Social Betterment," Felicity explained proudly.

Felicity was like her Aunt Hetty in that she loved big words, very proper behavior and organizations that gave a high tone to their members. Since Felicity couldn't find many such in Avonlea, she had decided to create her own.

Felix made another face, this time at Felicity.

"Who cares about your dumb ol' girls' meeting."

Felicity turned to the adults, exasperated. She really was, she felt, far too old to be sitting at a children's table with an irritating little brother.

"You see what I mean, Mother?"

"He'll be fine, Felicity," Janet told her quickly, not wanting any children's arguments at Sunday dinner.

"Alec, before we get into a domestic imbroglio," Hetty began, "shouldn't we...?"

"Oh, yes, yes, of course," exclaimed Alec, who then reached behind him and produced a carefully wrapped package. "Janet, Roger was looking through some of mother's things. He came across a box of very special mementos. Things that meant a great deal to mother and to the family. Hetty and Olivia insist that this go to you."

A King heirloom!

Janet, began to glow. "Oh. How kind of you!" she exclaimed as she began to unwrap the package with mounting anticipation. She knew how fussy the Kings were about their family treasures, and she could not help but be touched by the honor accorded her.

She pulled her gift from the wrapping paper—and fought to mask the shock and dismay on her face when she saw what was in her hand. The gift was a comb—a huge, hideously ornate comb, mother-of-pearl studded with great *faux* gems winking along its top. Heirloom or not, Janet thought it was just about the most garish, vulgar, tacky comb in the civilized world—and perhaps the uncivilized world as well.

All eyes were upon her, beaming in expectation of her joy at the lovely gift.

"Well, it's so very ... grand and ... *big*," Janet got out, desperately trying not to let her real feelings show.

Janet's opinion didn't seem to be shared by

anyone else. Felicity, especially, gazed at the comb as though she thought it was the most beautiful ornament she had ever laid eyes upon. "It's wonderful ..." she breathed, unable to take her eyes from the winking splendor in Janet's lap.

"It belonged to our great-grandmama," Hetty informed Janet, adding further sacred value to the object.

Privately, Janet thought that bad taste a hundred years ago was bad taste nonetheless, though she would never have dared hint such a thing aloud. King family feeling, she had learned over the course of her marriage, could be a very prickly and sensitive thing if offended by a wrong word from outsiders.

Hetty produced from her pocket a daguerreotype, a very old kind of photograph, of Great-Grandmama King. Its sepia-brown dimness showed a stern-looking middle-aged woman sitting straight as a fire poker and wearing the comb in her hair. Hetty handed it to Janet.

"This is the daguerreotype that she had done in New York City," Olivia explained proudly. "She was a very imposing woman, wasn't she?"

Janet King didn't know what to say. In her opinion, the woman looked to be a battle-ax of terrifying proportions.

Felicity strained to see the picture. "It makes her look so ... regal," she declared, her shoulders straightening to think that the magnificent woman in the picture was an ancestor of hers. Felicity was showing every sign of being a true King, through and through.

"Well, yes," Janet agreed, "but ... surely this is far too ... grand a gift to give to a mere relative-by-marriage? Alec?"

There was no way Janet was going to get out of owning the comb so easily. Her less-than-subtle appeal was completely misread. Alec, thinking his wife was only trying to be modest, smiled expansively.

"No, no, both Olivia and Hetty wanted you to have it, and I agree."

Not noticing Janet's grim look, the other two women at the table nodded happily. They were pleased with themselves for passing on such a generous gift to their sister-in-law. There seemed to be no help for it. Janet saw that she was truly stuck with the comb.

"I don't know how or when," she muttered through her teeth, "but I promise you I will repay your kindness."

Luckily, Janet's double meaning was lost upon her relatives.

Olivia lifted her glass with a flourish. "Well, to Great-Grandmama, then."

"Great-Grandmama," Hetty echoed, her eyes actually misty with the sentiment of the occasion.

They all drank to Great-Grandmama King's taste in jewelry. Then Alec began to hand out the other packages he had with him, the gifts he had purchased in Halifax for the children. Felix, Sara and Cecily ripped off the wrappings enthusiastically. Felicity, disapproving of the heedlessness of the others, removed the paper from her own gift with meticulous care. Already a thrifty young housekeeper, she was preserving the paper for future reuse.

Chapter Three

Later in the evening, Felicity sat in her bedroom in her nightclothes brushing her hair. As she brushed, she gazed at herself in the mirror and counted carefully. Ever since she had read that one hundred strokes a night caused hair to thicken and shine, Felicity had added the brushing to her bedtime routine, never skipping it, never cheating by stopping short before she had reached one hundred. Felicity was very proud of her wavy brown hair and dreamed of dressing it high on her head, the way the elegant society ladies did in the Charlottetown papers. She did not pause as Felix wandered in, reading a magazine.

"It says here," Felix informed her, "that if I rub my wart with a dead man's spit, it will miraculously vanish."

Even if a dead man's spit had been readily obtainable, this was hardly the sort of beauty tip Felicity had use for. She glowered at her brother's reflection in the mirror.

"I'm trying to count! Go away."

Cecily, who shared the room with Felicity, appeared at the door, happily clutching the new doll her father had brought back for her from Halifax. It had ribbons in its hair, a real china face and large, painted eyes that stared up adoringly. An identical doll lay on Felicity's bed, sprawled headfirst as though it had been pitched there in scorn.

"Why are you so cranky?" Felix grumbled. "Didn't you like father's gift?" Felix thought the magazine he'd gotten was terrifically entertaining.

Felicity made a face and yanked the brush through her hair.

"He brought me a *doll*!"

"Me too!" echoed Cecily in utter delight.

"Yes, but you're a child! You *like* dolls," Felicity spat disdainfully. "I'm a grown woman."

Since Felicity was only fourteen, this was a bit of an exaggeration. However, she was nearly fifteen, certainly beyond dolls, and she couldn't forgive her father for being so blind to her maturity as to bring her such a babyish toy.

Dolls had never been one of Felix's problems. Shrugging, he went back to his magazine.

"It says here that there is a tribe in Africa that can shrink heads down to the size of a baby's fist."

That was too much. Felicity yanked the magazine out of her brother's hands.

"*Secrets of the Occult*," she read, stabbing her brush at the lurid cover. "Why would Father buy you such trash?"

"You're just jealous 'cause you didn't like your present," Felix retorted, grabbing the magazine back while staying out of range of the hairbrush.

Felicity's eyes blazed, perhaps because Felix had hit rather too uncomfortably close to the mark. She began shooing her younger siblings out of the room, regardless of the fact that Cecily, at least, had a perfect right to be there.

"I think I should have gotten Great-Great-Grandmama's comb," she flung after them. "Mother just hasn't got the cheekbones for that sort of ornament."

"At least you got a present," Cecily pointed out. "Digger didn't get anything."

Unmoved by Digger's plight, Felicity slammed the door on her brother and sister and went back to tugging the brush hotly through her hair.

The next morning, Felicity hadn't forgotten the matter of her hair. The heirloom comb had danced through her dreams in the night, and she could not stop imagining how majestic she would look with such a glittering ornament perched atop her head.

As her mother, in the bedroom, got ready to go out, Felicity was at her like a terrier.

"Janet," Alec called upstairs from the kitchen. He was pacing the floor, impatient to get on the road.

"Yes, yes, Alec, I'm coming," Janet answered as she tried to do up the last of her buttons, bundle up baby Daniel and deal with her daughter at the same time.

She turned to Felicity. "Absolutely not," she insisted. "I'm sure none of the other girls in your consortium—"

"Colloquium," Felicity corrected, "for Social Betterment." Avonlea females needed a Colloquium for Social Betterment, if only to learn how to get the name right.

"Whatever ... the answer is no. You may not put your hair up."

When a girl was allowed to put her hair up and

let her skirts down, it was a sign that she was now a grown-up woman ready for courting. Janet wasn't letting any daughter of fourteen get away with that.

Tired of waiting downstairs, Alec had now come into the bedroom to see whether his presence would speed matters up. Doggedly, Felicity was making a last stand.

"But Mother, *you* aren't going to wear your new comb, and seeing as it is so beautiful ..."

"I said no. Besides, it's ..."—noticing Alec, she groped about for a diplomatic way to put it—"... my very special gift."

Thwarted on all sides, Felicity gave way to frustration and stamped her foot on the floor. She wanted nothing more in the world than to have her hair piled atop her head like an adult and that comb shimmering upon it.

"Mother! When are you and Father going to realize that I've grown up?"

"Perhaps when you quit stamping your feet," Janet returned dryly.

"I thought you were going to wear the comb today?" Alec said, looking rather pointedly at his wife.

Taken by surprise, Janet glanced away from her husband.

"Uh ... I thought that the Avonlea Sewing Circle was hardly the right place to unveil such a ... thing."

"Ah ... you wanted a more special occasion, is that it?"

Janet nodded, neglecting to tell her husband how very special the occasion would have to be to induce her to appear in public with that horror blinking atop her head. Before Alec could inquire any further, Janet hurried out, carrying the baby. Her husband followed at her heels.

Left behind, Felicity turned to the mirror on her mother's bureau and looked at herself critically, her hair falling in well-brushed brown waves down her back. Peeping towards the door to make sure she was alone, Felicity then piled her hair on top of her head and tried her best to look sophisticated.

When she heard the outside door slam, her mouth suddenly set into a defiant line. She began digging through her mother's drawers until she found, far at the back, all wrapped up in a cloth and thrust beneath some handkerchiefs, the precious comb itself. It was time to show who was really grown up.

That afternoon, in the King parlor, the Avonlea Young Women's Colloquium for Social Betterment awaited its hostess. Since this was the first meeting, the one that would establish the cultivated tone of the organization, all the girls present were dressed in their best, just as Felicity had requested. Sara Stanley was there, along with most of the other Avonlea girls Felicity went to school with, including Sally Potts, Clemmie Ray, Jane Spry and so on. All of them sat primly upright as they waited and examined each other's outfits with interest.

"Felicity wants us to talk about Avonlea's social ills," Sara said, by way of diverting thoughts from clothing to deeper things.

Clemmie Ray, who was probably the youngest, looked startled.

"Do we *have* any social ills?" she exclaimed, much surprised by the very idea.

Avonlea certainly did, Clemmie found out— and their source was in Clemmie's own family.

"Clemmie Ray, your brother Edward was seen swimming in the altogether. With nothing on!" Sally Potts elaborated, to make sure the chagrined girl understood.

"We saw him diving for turtles in Hodgin's Pond," Jane Spry confirmed, half smirking. "There was *lots* of naked boys there."

Sally and Jane were always in cahoots with each other, and if there was any mischief around Avonlea, the two were sure to be in on it. Sara, who had felt the sting of their taunts when she first arrived, was not on the best of terms with either of them. She shot them a critical look.

"It seems to me that spying is more a social ill than swimming," she said bluntly.

Before Jane or Sally could retort, Felicity came sailing into the room, stopping all conversation cold. Not only was she wearing her most handsome finery, she had her hair piled up on top of her head into a shining pyramid. And crowning the pyramid was the glittering arch of her mother's heirloom comb.

"Good afternoon!" she trilled airily.

Much to Felicity's annoyance and disappointment, no eager greetings, no cries of admiration, met her spectacular grand entrance. Her guests had been struck speechless, every one. Felicity waited, her cheeks coloring as the seconds ticked past. The effect she had hope to create was completely ruined by all the astonished stares.

"Close your mouths," Felicity finally snapped, "you look like a bunch of ignorant country girls."

"Felicity!" Sally Potts gasped.

"You look wonderful!" Clemmie Ray chimed in with belated but heartfelt enthusiasm. She had never in her life seen anything as pretty as that comb.

"Deportment is the first consideration of every

stylish young woman," Felicity told Clemmie, mollified a little and swiftly recovering her poise. "Now ladies, if you would please turn to your agendas ..."

Felicity was nothing if not organized. Each girl picked up the paper in front of her. Sara scanned it quickly, searching in vain for social ills.

"Are we really going to talk about hairstyles?" she asked, disappointed.

Apparently they were, for Felicity nodded. One of the advantages of being the founder of the Colloquium was the power to choose the themes of the meetings.

"Our first topic of discussion," Felicity announced, "is: 'The French Bob—Could It Happen Here?'"

"Certainly not!" Jane Spry exploded, immediately diverted from Felicity's comb. Even Jane, in rural Avonlea, knew that among the decadent Europeans, some women had taken to actually cutting off their hair. Avonlea girls could hardly imagine such an outrage.

"And why not?" Felicity inquired, fixing Jane with a challenging eye. As hostess, she meant to stimulate debate and even mobilize forces, if necessary, to keep the horrifying practice from reaching Canadian shores. You couldn't, after all, wear a jeweled comb on top of a French Bob.

"Because this is not France," Jane returned with scathing finality. Clearly, in her opinion, no Canadian woman would ever be debauched enough to take to the shears.

"What does the French Bob have to do with social ills?" Sara demanded. She did not feel personally threatened, as Felicity seemingly did, by any menace to her locks. She thought the Colloquium could find more serious problems closer to home.

"I don't know," muttered Jane, "but I wouldn't be caught dead in one."

The subject died into a rather uncomfortable silence, with no answer offered to Sara's question. As Sara began to look bored and restless, Felicity realized that running her Colloquium smoothly was going to be tougher than she thought. Inexplicably, the perils of the French Bob had failed to rivet the girls to their seats. She had better rush on to the next gripping topic before her squirming guests started thinking about open revolt.

Chapter Four

Over at Lawson's general store, the Avonlea Sewing Circle was getting together. Lawson's was a sort of informal social center for the village.

Sooner or later, everyone in Avonlea came in to buy something and stayed to chat. The best bits of gossip were heard first at the store, and anyone who passed through the village could be remarked upon from its wide front windows. It was only natural that the women should range themselves in chairs beside the iron stove and settle in to hear the latest.

"What news did Alec bring of Halifax, Janet?" Mrs. Potts was asking. Clara Potts was Sally's mother. She had the loosest tongue in Avonlea and was always avid for any little tidbit to keep ahead of local gossip.

Hetty King was also there, along with Rachel Lynde and Mrs. Lawson, who had the added advantage of being able to socialize and watch her store at the same time. Though they all had a bit of sewing in their hands, a meeting of the Avonlea Sewing Circle was more of an excuse for the women to visit with each other than a time to do any actual needlework.

"Oh, not much, Clara," Janet replied, knowing no move of the Kings would escape Mrs. Potts. "He and his brother Roger spent most of their time digging through old junk."

Janet had phrased this rather badly. Hetty's head shot up.

"Heirlooms, I think you mean, Janet!" she corrected sharply. After all, King family property could hardly be described as "old junk."

Rachel Lynde nodded knowingly and shifted her stout form more comfortably into her chair. "Well some family pass-me-downs are worth quite a lot of money," she said.

Hetty thoroughly agreed. "In point of fact, a few treasures were uncovered," she told her companions with a tantalizing air.

"Like my new comb?" Janet was trying mightily to keep the sarcasm out of her voice.

"Great-Grandmama's comb." Sewing forgotten, Hetty folded her hands in her lap. Her eyes went misty. "Now, there's a story. Whilst the Americans were attacking Fort George during the War of 1812, you know, Great-Grandmama was loading muskets. Just when defeat seemed imminent, Creat Grandmama seized a musket and, employing her considerable marksmanship, turned the tide against the marauding Yankees. POW! POW! POW!" Hetty startled her listeners considerably with a good simulation of musket fire. "Her long, beautiful, raven hair kept falling forward on the flintlock, until a dashing young captain came to the rescue and tied it back with a leather thong. Thus, when Fort George was saved, Great-Grandmama was presented with the very comb which is now bestowed upon our Janet."

Hetty finished up with a flourish, glowing with the heroic exploits of her ancestor. According to Hetty, Great-Grandmama had saved the fort singlehandedly. Trust Hetty, Janet thought, not to miss any opportunity to aggrandize the Kings.

"Hetty, if my history serves me," Janet couldn't resist correcting, "Fort George did fall to the Americans."

Hetty's nostrils flared. Clara Potts eyed Janet with newfound curiosity.

"Why aren't you wearing the comb now, Janet?" Clara asked, instinctively hitting Janet's sore spot. Ferreting out matters better left at rest was Clara's special talent.

"Perhaps I shall," Janet returned, "if marauding Yankees ever attack Avonlea."

Everyone laughed, except Hetty, who was still smarting about being caught out in her tale about Fort George. Schoolteachers weren't supposed to tamper with history, no matter how much to their own advantage. And now here was Janet, a mere relative by marriage, making light of the hallowed heirloom comb.

Before Hetty could form a reproof to that effect, the store door opened. Reverend Fitzsimmons

poked his head in from the street, evidently bent
on pursuing his pastoral duties.

"Good afternoon, ladies." He insinuated himself a little further in, though not quite far enough
to actually join the female conclave. "I couldn't
help overhearing your laughter, and that brought
to mind Ecclesiastes, chapter seven, verse five." As
though unable to help himself, he suddenly broke
into his preaching voice. "'It is better to hear the
rebuke of the wise than for a man to hear the song
of fools.' Good day."

With that totally unexpected volley of biblical
enlightenment, he disappeared again, leaving the
women with their sewing forgotten and their
mouths open.

"Song of fools," spluttered Hetty. "If you ask
me, a little too much inspiration sinks into his
vocal cords from time to time."

Janet couldn't help grinning. Maybe the minister had overheard Hetty's fanciful speech about
Fort George.

"Perhaps," she quipped, "we should have told
him to go fly a kite."

A wave of irreverent giggles overtook the
women, which they decently tried to stifle as best
they could.

Back at the King farmhouse, Felicity's meeting was still in session—or rather dragging endlessly on. Once the threat of the French Bob had been discussed and disposed of, Felicity had moved on to the science of personal hair care. In this, she considered herself quite an expert, though her audience seemed not at all impressed. In fact, the other girls squirmed in their chairs, yawned openly and stared longingly out the window. Everyone looked bored to stupefaction by Felicity's talk.

"...and now you can see the importance of the 'Rule of One Hundred Strokes: toothbrush and hairbrush.'" She paused and waited for a reaction. "Well? Ladies?" she prompted impatiently when no one moved.

Her only answer was assorted stomach rumbles.

"Felicity," groaned Sara, "if we don't eat soon, I shall drop dead."

The others bobbed their heads in wholehearted agreement. Felicity had to accept the inevitable, even though they weren't yet a quarter of the way through the ambitious agenda she had planned. She sighed and rang a small brass bell at her side.

"Cecily! Felix!" she called out. "You can now bring in the refreshments." Then she turned to the other girls. "I wish you would all try to concentrate," she told them reproachfully, the very weight of the comb in her hair making her feel infinitely more mature than all the rest put together.

Cecily and Felix, who had been recruited as kitchen staff, lugged in a huge tray holding glasses of milk and covered with cookies and small cakes. If nothing else, Felicity was an excellent cook and had worked hard to do things up right in the refreshment department. All the girls brightened at the sight.

Felix, who was participating only under extreme coercion, spotted Felicity's crowning glory right away. He went on the attack.

"I thought mother said you couldn't wear that comb," he announced, hoping to embarrass his sister.

Felicity glared at her brother and hurried to continue with her program. Matters to do with hair, she felt vehemently, were none of Felix's business.

"Next on our agenda is posture and profile."

"How about the posture and profile of Edward Ray?" Sally Potts cooed, sending the rest of the girls, except Felicity, into giggles.

Felicity began to get truly steamed.

"This is *hardly* the level of discourse the Avonlea Young Women's Colloquium for Social —"

"Was Thomas Nisbet there?" Clemmie asked breathlessly, cutting Felicity off.

"Do you *like* Thomas Nisbet?" Jane Spry wanted

to know. She could hardly believe it! Thomas had freckles, even on his neck, and eyelashes so pale you could hardly see them.

Felicity clapped her hands sharply to stop the snickering. Her fine, altruistic meeting was breaking up before her eyes.

"You know what you sound like? Geese! A bunch of silly geese."

Felix took advantage of the distraction to snatch up a cookie. Felicity slapped him on the wrist.

"What are you doing? Help eats in the kitchen," she seethed, repossessing the stolen item. Then she turned back to the girls in a last-ditch attempt to reestablish order. "Now, posture and profile are vital to a Good First Impression—"

While Felicity's head was turned, Felix mutinously grabbed a whole handful of cookies. He had been nettled by the slap. And if the help had to eat in the kitchen, then he was determined that the help should at least eat well.

"You know, it's not fair," put in Jane Spry, ignoring Felicity. "Can you imagine if *we* decided to swim uncovered?"

"I said stop it," Felicity snapped at Felix, making a futile attempt to recover the goodies. She hadn't slaved over a hot oven only to have everything gobbled by a greedy little brother.

Gripping his booty tighter, Felix skipped out of reach.

"I've been waiting an hour and a half in that stuffy old kitchen while you talked and talked and talked, boring everyone to death."

"No one was bored!" Felicity spun round to the other girls for vindication. "Was anyone bored?"

She was met by a wall of glazed expressions that said it all. Much piqued, Felicity made a grab at her brother and managed to get a cookie back. Then Felix seized it again. In an instant, the cookie was crushed to crumbs in the tug of war. Felix slammed into the table that the tray sat on and it overturned with a crash, sending milk and cookies everywhere. Felicity stared, appalled, at the mess on her mother's best carpet.

"That's it, you wretched boy!" she shrieked, flying at Felix in a fury.

Knowing he was really in trouble, Felix bolted from the room, his now completely undone sister in raging pursuit.

The remaining girls gawked at the smashed cakes lying at their feet. Sara's mouth twitched irreverently.

"Now I'm not bored," she told the others with a grin.

Chapter Five

Felix raced out of the house and charged across the yard, yelling for help as he ran. Felicity scorched along at his heels, all her grown-up dignity tossed aside in her determination to catch the cookie-thieving culprit. Driven by fear, Felix actually made it all the way over the grass and into the barn before Felicity cornered him beside the calf pen. She was bigger, older and faster, and she was going to use every advantage she had. Without a second's hesitation, she lunged at Felix in a running tackle and captured him, up against the feed sacks, in a headlock rigid as iron.

"Leave me alone," Felix bellowed, struggling in vain to escape. Felicity was cutting off his wind and mashing his tender earlobes into his skull.

"What have you got to say now?" Felicity demanded heatedly. She felt about ready to murder her brother for ruining her refined meeting.

All Felix did was struggle harder for his own release. "Let go of me!" he squawked, trying to bite Felicity's arm.

Felicity, veteran of many such struggles, hadn't the least intention of giving up her superiority. On the other hand, she couldn't exactly keep Felix in a headlock for the rest of the afternoon—

at least not while she was wearing her best merino dress. For penance, she decided to make Felix grovel very low.

"Repeat after me: 'I am a loathsome, boorish *squid.'"*

Felix writhed harder, trying for a lucky escape.

"Ow! Let go!"

"Say it! Say it!" Felicity ordered, tightening her grip on Felix's neck.

Starved for oxygen, Felix could feel his resistance weakening.

"I am a loathsome, boorish—some kind of sea creature?"

"A loathsome, boorish squid," Felicity insisted, squeezing Felix like a python to make him obey.

Felix held out as long as he could, pulling and tugging at Felicity's relentless grip.

"I am a loathsome, boorish squid," he finally gasped out, just as he began to see big yellow spots before his eyes.

Triumphantly, Felicity released her brother. Even though she herself was now bedraggled, dirty and mussed, she had won. Her hair now tumbled every which way but she hardly noticed. Her face was still flushed from the fray.

"That'll teach you to ruin my afternoon!" she ground out, her eyes blazing with the memory of the overturned table and Felix's utter uselessness as a waiter.

Felix, too busy doing his best to catch his breath and recover some dignity, didn't bother to answer.

When Felicity finally reached up to tidy her coiffure, she felt around frantically on top of her head, then froze. Great-Great-Grandmama's comb, so firmly stuck into her topknot, was missing!

"It's gone!" she squawked. "Mother's beautiful comb is gone! Find it! We have to find it!"

Without a thought for her dress, Felicity dropped to her knees and started digging around in the hay that surrounded her.

Felix, who could be forgiven for not making the slightest attempt to help, cheered up instantly at this turn of events.

"That comb is worth a fortune Felicity—and you lost it!" He laughed aloud, rubbing it in. If Felicity hadn't been so anxious to find the comb she certainly would have jumped up and squeezed his head for him again.

The disaster spelled a rapid end to the first meeting of the Avonlea Young Women's Colloquium for Social Betterment. Denied refreshments, and fearing more from Felicity on the subject of profiles and posture, the members slipped out the front door and dispersed as quickly as they could.

Felicity was actually glad to see them go. Their departure left her relatives free to be recruited into the search. As soon as she could, she had Sara and Felix out in the barn again rooting around in the hay. The hay didn't seem to have any heirloom combs in it, but it did have plenty of dust and cobwebs and prickly seeds. Very shortly, the children looked much the worse for wear, with grimy knees, rumpled clothes and mats of chaff in their hair. Only Cecily and Digger seemed to have escaped the furor. They came in quietly through the barn door.

"It's not here," Sara concluded, tossing a last armful of fodder to the floor. "Maybe we should check the yard again."

Felix, who had joined the search mainly to enjoy his sister's discomfiture, grinned impudently.

"Face it, Felicity, you'll be imprisoned in your room—forever."

Felicity was getting desperate enough to believe him. She quaked at the collective fury that would descend upon her when her parents found out. She could not escape the fact that she had broken express orders not to wear the comb and was headed for dire punishment over its loss.

"Look again!" she begged, unable to believe

that the large, mother-of-pearl-inlaid comb could simply evaporate into thin air.

"The others went home," Cecily told her sister unnecessarily. "They had enough social betterment for one day."

Sara tried to brush stalks of hay off her dress and examined its torn hem. It was a dress her father had bought her in Paris, and it didn't look as though the edging could be stitched back on again without showing the mend.

"Can't you just tell Aunt Janet you're sorry?"

The mere suggestion dragged a ragged breath from Felicity.

"Sara, it's an heirloom! The gift of that comb means the world to Mother." With Felicity, as with Aunt Hetty, reverence for family treasures ran deep.

"I bet it's worth a lot of money," Felix added, twisting the screw a little tighter.

At this, Felicity broke down completely. Putting her hands to her face she began sobbing aloud. In a rather useless effort to be comforting, Sara patted her shoulder.

"Don't worry, Felicity, it will show up."

"I betcha it won't," Felix jibed with heartless glee. "Betcha Felicity will be in trouble for *years* over this one." Felicity might have won a battle with her brother, but in doing so, she had driven

him to declare all-out war. He meant to jab merci-
lessly whenever he saw an opening.

"I just want to be there when Mother and
Father find out!"

Driven beyond endurance, Felicity snatched
up a pitchfork and aimed it at her brother's
heart.

"Mother and Father aren't going to find out,
Felix. It could be months before she decides to
wear that comb."

"You can't keep it a secret!" exclaimed Sara,
shocked. "Don't you remember what Reverend
Fitzsimmons said about sins and piranhas?"

Felicity seemed quite willing to risk a whole
horde of toothy sins if only she could keep this
catastrophe quiet. She pressed the tines of the
pitchfork to Felix's chest.

"Promise me, Felix! You will not say a word to
Mother or Father about the comb. Promise me or
I'll run you through."

With her hair trailing in her eyes and straw
sticking out of her dress, she looked crazy enough
to mean it. Remembering the headlock, Felix
didn't quite have the nerve to challenge the wild-
ness in his sister's eye.

"I promise," he grunted, without the least bit of
sincerity.

"Spit on your hand," Felicity ordered, the pitchfork unmoving.

Felix spat on his hand, his eye on the gleaming metal tines.

"Now rub it on your heart!"

"That's disgusting," Felix protested, making a face.

Needing to extract the most fearsome oath she could think of, Felicity raised the pitchfork higher. Felix reached into his shirt and, grimacing, rubbed the spit over his heart.

Sara threw up her hands in frustration. "Didn't either of you listen to a word the Reverend said?"

Chapter Six

Unfortunately for Felicity, it wasn't months before her mother decided to wear the heirloom comb. Bombarded by hints from her husband, Janet made up her mind to display the thing that very Sunday at church, if only in the interests of marital peace. With the expectant and easily offended King clan mollified, Janet hoped she would be off the hook. Then, perhaps, the frightful comb could stay out of sight in a drawer until it was time for another unfortunate in-law to be stuck with it.

But first, she had to find the thing!

Sunday mornings were always rushed, with breakfast and chores and then everyone having to get dressed for church. Alec, in his collar and tie, had gone out to the barn to hitch up the horse and buggy. Now the buggy stood outside, all ready to go while Alec waited in the kitchen.

"Janet, don't forget to wear your new comb," he called upstairs to his wife, just in case she needed a reminder.

Janet was in their bedroom scrabbling through a drawer in search of the ornament that was to be her crowning glory for the day.

"Oh, for heaven's sake, I know we're late."

Janet had expected to put her hand on the comb instantly and thrust it into her hair as she rushed out. Now she pulled open yet another drawer and hurriedly turned over its contents.

Felicity, hearing the commotion and fearing the worst, appeared at the bedroom door. When she saw what her mother was doing, she began to look very apprehensive.

"You don't know where my new comb is, do you?" Janet asked, tossing the dreaded question over her shoulder.

Alarm shot into Felicity's face. She clenched her hands into fists against her skirt.

"Uh ... I haven't the slightest inkling of where it could be ... right now."

This stammered answer was, in the strictest sense, quite true. Luckily, Janet didn't notice the trickiness of Felicity's grammar. She rummaged in the drawer again, much flustered.

"I swear I left it in here, but what with the baby and all... Let's get going, then. I'll find it another time."

Janet was secretly pleased at this reprieve. Besides, who knew what that strange Reverend Fitzsimmons would do to anyone daring to arrive after the service had started.

Janet slammed the drawer shut and abandoned the search, leaving Felicity quite shaky with relief. Without another word, Janet hurried downstairs to join her husband. As quickly as they could, the whole family bundled into the buggy and set off.

Inside the small Avonlea church, Rachel Lynde was, as usual, pumping away at the organ. Reverend Fitzsimmons, fiery-eyed, was leading the congregation in a hymn of his choosing, entitled, rather ominously, "Thou Judge of Quick and Dead." Reverberating under the wooden ceiling, the verses lived up to their title.

Thou Judge of quick and dead,
Before whose bar severe,
With holy joy or guilty dread,
We all shall soon appear.

Reverend Fitzsimmons belted out the words with gusto, followed, as best they could, by the rest of the congregation. Hetty, Sara and Olivia were prominent among them.

The singing, for all its loudness, hardly covered the entrance of the King family. Despite the best efforts of the horse, Janet's fruitless search had made them late after all.

As the latecomers hurried to get into their seats, Hetty and Sara were somewhat unceremoniously shunted along to make room. Hetty was not pleased to be jostled around inside her own pew by tardy relatives. Nor was she happy to discover Alec and Janet so wrapped up in an argument that they were oblivious to just how far their whispers carried. Hetty and Olivia overheard them, along with Felix and Felicity and practically everyone else in the church.

"But you said you'd wear it this week," Alec was claiming, eyes fixed on his wife's unadorned head.

"I decided it really wasn't a church sort of comb," Janet tossed back, grabbing the first excuse she could think of. She couldn't very well tell her husband that she hadn't been able to find the blessed thing.

"Great-Grandmama wore it to my christening," Alec informed her in reproachful tones.

If Alec thought this increased the comb's value for Janet, he was much mistaken. Janet barely controlled her temper.

"Shush, Alec!"

The latecomers finally settled themselves, just in time to see Reverend Fitzsimmons stride purposefully across to the pulpit. That item of furnishing had been shored up, in anticipation of the Reverend's fist-thumping sermon, with some sturdy, if unsightly, pieces of timber.

The minister squared his shoulders, planted both feet wide and stared down into the congregation. He stared so long that they all began to squirm uncomfortably. By now, they all knew they were in for a scorching blast. A number gripped the edge of their pews to brace themselves.

"AND AT THAT AWFUL HOUR THE ARCHANGEL'S VOICE WILL DEAFEN US," he suddenly bellowed, making the entire congregation jump in their seats, "CRYING 'YE DEAD THE JUDGE IS COME! ARISE AND MEET YOUR INSTANT DOOM!'"

Despite the young minister's very creditable imitation of the archangel, Alec could not get his mind off the comb.

"I'd think you'd be proud to wear such a fine King family heirloom ..." he whispered to his wife.

By now Hetty also had noticed the glaring absence atop Janet's hair, and she joined her brother in the attack.

"The Wards never could recognize quality," Hetty said into the air, quite loud enough for Janet to hear.

Janet had been a Ward before her marriage. Her temper flared instantly, as it always did when the Kings gave themselves airs over the Wards.

"And the Kings think quality is measured by glitter alone!" she slung back heatedly. Considering the awful garishness of the comb, she didn't think Hetty had much of a leg to stand on when discussing taste.

By this time, the King family quarrel had become obvious to the other members of the congregation. Elvira Lawson stopped listening to the minister and leaned forward to catch what the Kings were saying. Hank Webster, in front, turned right around in his seat in an attempt to listen in. A number of others cocked their ears as best they could. Even the Archangel Gabriel couldn't com-

pete with the spectacle of the respectable Kings
going at it hammer and tongs.

"THAT DAY OF RECKONING WILL COME!"
Reverend Fitzsimmons boomed out. "WILL YE BE
CAST INTO THE LAKE OF UNENDING FIRE
WHICH BURNS AND BURNS AND DOES NOT
CONSUME?"

The terrible words bombarded Felicity. She
gasped in outright fear as her brother poked her in
the ribs.

"Lake of fire!" Felix hissed, gleefully emphasizing
the horrible fate awaiting those who lost heirloom
combs.

And Hetty, as though ganging up with the
archangel to further remind Felicity of her sins,
said, in the general direction of Janet, "That comb
is a hundred years old."

By now Mrs. Potts was practically popping
her dress buttons as she twisted round to catch
the King drama, while her husband, unmoved by
either archangels, Kings or noisy ministers, snoozed
beside her.

Of all the people there, Felicity seemed to be
the only one drinking in every word Reverend
Fitzsimmons said. Everyone else, save for those
few asleep, was watching to see what Janet or Alec
would do next.

From his vantage point in the pulpit, the minister could not help but notice the distraction of his congregation. He compensated by upping his volume even more.

"LOOK AT YOUR SOULS!" he thundered, twisting his boyish, pink face into an attempt at a terrifying scowl. "ARE THEY AS CRYSTAL GOBLETS RINGING WITH THE HIGH HARMONIC SOUND OF VIRTUE? OR AS SCULLERY POTS, BLACKENED BY COMMON USAGE, DIRTY AND DENTED?"

"Yes, every Thanksgiving we would pass the comb around the table," Alec mused, full of memories and apparently not concerned about the number of dents in his soul.

Attacked from both sides, Janet was becoming undone by this family onslaught. Her cheeks were growing redder, and it was taking all of her self-control to keep herself in check.

"We intended it as an affectionate gesture, Janet," Hetty pointed out, "giving you the comb."

"Well ... it was, of course," Janet muttered through her teeth. No amount of backtracking was going to make her forget the comment about the Wards.

"THE LORD LOOKS DOWN UPON US AND WEEPS," brayed Reverend Fitzsimmons. "DECEIT!

VANITY! GREED! THE END IS NIGH! SAITH THE LORD GOD."

Felicity's attention was riveted on the minister. Everything he said was true. Deceit and vanity *had* led her astray—right to the brink of the burning pit! Her eyes widened as she imagined the flames sizzling around her.

"The end is nigh!" she echoed mournfully, unaware that she was repeating the dreadful words aloud.

"AND ON THAT TERRIBLE DAY, A THIRD OF THE MOON WILL BE STRUCK AND THE ANGEL GABRIEL WILL DESCEND FROM HEAVEN TO WARN THE RIGHTEOUS. WILL YOU BE THERE? WILL YOU BE WALKING...?"

The minister's loudness became less effective as more and more people learned to turn off the noise. Deaf to the calamitous events being predicted from the pulpit, Olivia now took up the problem of the missing comb. Being of a more peaceable nature than her prickly sister, she tried another tack.

"We do admire you, you know, Janet," she explained. "We wanted to show that in some small way. We wanted you to feel like—"

"Like a King!" Hetty thrust in bluntly. "Go on, say it, Olivia."

"Like a King!" Olivia repeated, unable to think of any other way to phrase it.

"Foolish us to think that was possible." Hetty barreled on, completely spoiling Olivia's attempt at diplomacy. Then, spying the fascination of Mrs. Potts, Hetty glared in that woman's direction. "Clara!" she admonished, in her sharpest school-teacher voice.

Her reproof was drowned by the good Reverend, who roared "REPENT!" in a voice that shook the windows. By now, he was quite carried away with his efforts to save his flock from certain perdition. "ASK FORGIVENESS! DISAVOW YOUR WEAK SPIRIT AND COMMEND YOURSELF TO FINAL JUDGMENT."

Janet ignored him. She felt she was being subjected to enough final judgment right then and there—especially when her own husband had joined the forces ranged against her.

"Grandmother would wear that comb to every family wedding and funeral," Alec remembered, looking as though he suspected Grandmother had slept with it on, too.

"How do you think that makes us feel, Janet?" Hetty demanded, pressing her fingers to her bodice as though wounded to the heart by her sister-in-law's negligence.

"WHERE WILL WE HIDE FROM GABRIEL'S TRUMPET?" Reverend Fitzsimmons asked from the pulpit.

"I have no idea!" Janet answered under her breath.

"It came to be a symbol of the courage of all King women," Hetty went on.

"WILL YOU BE CRUSHED AND CAST AWAY?" blared the sermon. "NOW IS THE TIME, PEOPLE OF AVONLEA, FOR A REASSESSMENT OF YOUR LIVES. JUDGMENT DAY IS AT HAND."

Felicity paled, as though expecting the Archangel Gabriel to crash in through the roof at any moment. She imagined herself hauled before a heavenly tribunal and grilled about the comb.

"And we wanted you to display that courage," Alec went on, unaware of just how much grit it would have taken for Janet to actually wear the gaudy decoration.

Olivia and Hetty nodded in perfect agreement. The King family seemed ranged solidly against Janet. She sighed in resignation.

"Very well. If courage is what it takes to wear that comb, I'll try to measure up."

Just as Janet said this, the Reverend Fitzsimmons expelled a mighty breath and came to the end of his sermon. At once, he deflated to his normal size and voice and turned towards the organ.

"Now, Mrs. Lynde, if you would be so kind as to play hymn number 247."

Under Rachel Lynde's energetic hands, the instrument wheezed to life. The congregation responded with a startled scramble for their hymnbooks and, after much fumbling, found their places. Voices straggling behind the music, they began to sing. The only one who remained silent was Felicity. She was too frightened and too moved by the sermon to open her mouth.

After the hymn and the benediction, the service finally ground to an end. Reverend Fitzsimmons took up his position outside the church door to shake hands with the congregation.

Outside, Felicity caught up with Sara, Cecily and Felix.

"Felicity! Are you well?" Sara asked, startled by her cousin's sickly pallor.

Felix made a mocking face. He understood why Felicity looked so green about the gills.

"Felicity knows *her* soul is like a black, dented old pot."

"How could anyone possibly be well after that sermon?" Felicity quavered, bravely attempting to recover herself.

"I wasn't listening to the sermon," Sara told

them. "I was listening to your parents argue about the comb."

"*Everyone* was arguing," said Felix. "I heard Mrs. Lawson say that Mother was ungrateful."

No one needed to tell Felicity about the family quarrel—or about who was responsible for all the trouble. Between the sermon and the argument, Felicity was completely unnerved.

"Reverend Fitzsimmons knows," she groaned, certain her guilt had been emblazoned on her forehead for the good man to see. "He was looking directly at me through the whole sermon."

Sara, who also knew all about Felicity's agonies and thought them much exaggerated, shrugged her shoulders. The answer seemed obvious.

"You're all upset and silly. Why don't you just take your medicine?"

"Because if I could just find the comb everything would be fine," Felicity answered, still clinging, even in the face of the Archangel Gabriel, to this last hope. The anger of her parents over the vanished comb would be bad enough, but the wrath of her Aunt Hetty, should the lofty symbol of King womanhood and courage be lost, made Felicity quail where she stood. She could not be blamed for trying, even at risk of the fiery pit, to solve the problem herself.

Chapter Seven

Much later, at Rose Cottage, Hetty and Olivia were gathering up the plates after a light supper. Sara sat nearby, curled up in an armchair, paging laboriously through a heavy, leather-bound book. Even here, in the cozy kitchen long after the church service, the two women were still in a state about the unworn comb.

"Those Wards never had a sense of history," Hetty sniffed as she poured hot water from the kettle into the dishpan. "That's the problem."

Olivia, who usually attempted to moderate Hetty's more extreme opinions, was in total agreement this time. In fact, if anything, she was even more worked up than her sister. Of a romantic turn of mind, Olivia couldn't imagine why anyone would refuse to wear a comb ennobled by a fierce battle with the Yankees and passed reverently from hand to hand down to the present lucky owner.

"When I was a girl, I admired Great-Grandmama more than anyone else in the family. Hetty, it has nothing to do with a sense of history. Oh, if I'd known Janet was going to feel that way, I'd have kept the comb myself."

"That's enough, Olivia," Hetty interjected,

belatedly trying to be fair. "Janet's promised to fulfil her familial obligation, so ..."

"Only after we bullied her into it. You'd think she'd be proud to wear such a gift," Olivia stormed on, unappeased by Janet's obviously grudging promise.

Sara, who knew perfectly well why her Aunt Janet hadn't worn the comb, listened with increasing discomfort. Finally, unable to keep silent any longer, she took it upon herself to try to save her aunt from more of the unjust battering.

"I'm sure Aunt Janet never intended to cause such an uproar," she asserted. "I'm sure she'd be happy to wear it to a special occasion like ... like a ball."

Since there were exceedingly few balls in Avonlea, Sara thought this might save her aunt, at least until the comb was found.

Hetty plunged her hands impatiently into the dishwater. "Oh Sara, don't make excuses for her," she blustered, swinging back to Olivia's side now that someone else was attempting to excuse Janet.

Gallantly, Sara stuck to her guns.

"But wasn't the whole point that you gave it to her as a gift?" she argued. "Now you're all badgering her about it. It just doesn't seem fair. Maybe she had a good reason not to wear it."

"Like what?" Olivia wanted to know, her lips pursed tight.

Sara was saved from that touchy question by Hetty, who now changed sides again and bristled at her sister.

"Now you're badgering Sara! Really, Olivia, it'll do no good to stew about it. Janet will wear the comb in her own good time."

"While we're all alive and breathing, I hope," Olivia added darkly as she attacked the dripping plates with the dish towel.

The matter died away for the moment while the dishes were finished and put away. In the interval, Hetty finally noticed Sara's stillness and the size of the grim-looking volume she had in her lap.

"Sara, what are you doing?" Hetty asked.

"I'm trying to answer a question."

"What question?"

As the Avonlea schoolteacher and local expert on matters intellectual, Hetty felt she ought to have been consulted first if Sara needed an answer to a question.

"About the world. About when it began and when it'll end," Sara said matter-of-factly.

Hetty stopped with a handful of plates halfway to the cupboard. This was a bit more philosophy than Rose Cottage was accustomed to, and certainly not the sort of question Hetty had been expecting.

"End? Wherever did you get such an outlandish notion?" she rapped out, revealing that she hadn't heard a word of Reverend Fitzsimmons's sermon.

"Hetty, can't she even ask a simple question?" Olivia broke in, still spoiling for a fight. "I mean, obviously if the world began at some point in time, it's logically going to end."

"You've been talking to Jasper too long, Olivia," Hetty told her sister tartly. Olivia's husband, besides being a bit of an inventor, was very interested in all manner of strange scientific questions. A number of times, Jasper had managed to make quite a laughingstock out of himself in his efforts to prove one or another of his pet theories. Needless to say, the down-to-earth folk around Avonlea tended to think him very eccentric and just a little mad.

"Felix has been scaring Felicity half to death," Sara revealed, "because the Reverend Fitzsimmons mentioned it in his sermon. I'm just trying to prove it won't happen."

Oh well, if that was all that was at the root of the problem, thought Hetty, it was hardly worth bothering about. She turned back to emptying the dishpan. Like a great many other practical folk, Hetty saw no reason to rack her brain over abstractions nobody could put a provable answer to.

"Never mind, child," she told Sara with firm assurance. "If the world does end, it certainly won't be in my lifetime or yours."

Over at the King farmhouse, a more immediate problem was harrying the inhabitants—or harrying two of them, anyway. What's more, neither dared let the other know what the trouble was.

Janet King, pretending to dust, was lifting vases and turning over books, doing her best to find the comb. Felicity, on her hands and knees poking about under the furniture, was doing exactly the same thing. Each was trying to hide her efforts from the other.

"What are you doing, Felicity?" Janet asked, wondering why on earth her normally dignified daughter was crawling about on the floor.

"I dropped some jacks," Felicity fabricated hastily. "They spilled everywhere."

Janet wasn't happy having a witness to her anxious exertions—but how to get Felicity out of the house?

"Felicity, would you get me some eggs?"

"Pardon?"

"I asked you to please get me some eggs."

"But I collected eggs this morning!" Felicity protested, wondering whether her mother had taken leave of her senses.

"Ðon't argue with me, young lady, I'm feeling dangerous," Janet cried, desperate to get Felicity out of the room so she could look under the furniture herself. After the episode in the church, Janet either had to find the comb or risk getting court martialled by the Kings.

Reluctantly, Felicity headed off towards the chicken coop, knowing full well there would be no eggs. After the minister's thundering sermon, the lost comb weighed horribly on her conscience. Every moment she spent away from her search was a torture to her.

Blissfully oblivious to the problems of the womenfolk, Alec King was treating himself to a pleasant afternoon hunting rabbits. As he tramped through the woods, his gun over his shoulder, he wasn't much of a threat to the wildlife. What he really liked was just being out in the fresh air, with the breeze in the branches overhead and the mysterious, earthy smell of the forest in his nostrils.

Consequently, he was more than a little startled to hear forceful shouts coming in bursts, like cannon fire, through the trees. Thinking, from the sound of it, that somebody must be in terrible trouble, Alec broke into a run to investigate. As he came closer to the source of the noise, he identified it, with astonishment, as the voice of Reverend Fitzsimmons, bellowing at the top of his lungs.

"AND JACOB WRESTLED WITH THE ANGEL AND WRESTLED UNTIL DAWN," the minister was bawling at a flock of sparrows, "YET HE COULD NOT PREVAIL!"

Alec pushed close enough to see that the good Reverend, though quite alone, was engaged in such strange contortions that he might very well have been wrestling an invisible angel of his own. Supposing the fellow in the throes of some kind of fit, Alec rushed forward in alarm—only to discover that the minister really *was* wrestling with an angel.

The crazy dance the man was performing was his way of flying a huge kite. And on that kite the Archangel Gabriel was vividly painted, horn, robe and all. After the blazing sermon in the church, a casual observer could be forgiven for thinking that the minister was flying the kite, like bait, towards Heaven, in an effort to encourage the real Archangel Gabriel to stop dawdling with Judgment Day.

"AND LO—THE ANGEL OF THE LORD WAS MIGHTY AND—"

Alec was unable to stop his rush in time to make a diplomatic exit—or even a diplomatic entrance. "Reverend Fitzsimmons!" was all he could exclaim as he burst from a stand of poplars into the open space.

Fitzsimmons was so surprised that he released the kite, tripped and fell backward, striking his head on a nearby oak. The knock seemed to stun him, for he slumped to the ground, quite limp. The kite made a complete escape, flying off through the air with Gabriel's robe billowing in the breeze and his horn raised, ready to sound the very trump of doom.

Alec raced forward and grasped the minister by the shoulder. By the time he had him propped up against the tree, the Reverend was struggling to rub at his bruised head. He grasped at the flask Alec pulled from his pocket to offer him.

"That's it. Here we go," Alec encouraged, hoping to swiftly revive the fellow.

Even in his dazed condition, Reverend Fitzsimmons didn't forget his principles. Before he drank, he sniffed delicately at the flask.

"Don't worry, it's only water," Alec assured him, stifling a grin.

Fitzsimmons nodded and took a grateful gulp.

"Thank you, Mr. King."

The water seemed to restore the minister quite as much as demon liquor might have done a less virtuous man.

"I'm sorry I startled you like that." Alec stopped short of mentioning that shouting clergymen were not quite what he was accustomed to meeting on a rabbit hunt.

Fitzsimmons took another swig from the flask and fingered the bump on his head.

"Oh, I was engrossed in next week's sermon: 'Jacob and the Angel.'"

"I'm afraid your kite is probably on its way to Africa," Alec observed ruefully, gesturing at the dot receding in the empty sky.

Fitzsimmons shrugged. "I've got quite a few of them, actually."

"Do you ... do you normally fly them in the dead of winter?"

"Neither rain, nor snow, nor sleet, nor hail can stop the truly devoted, Mr. King," the minister replied dauntlessly. "I find the making and flying of kites very fulfilling."

"Sort of a fishing line to Heaven, is it?" Alec chuckled, enormously relieved that the minister was all right.

"Yes, exactly, Mr. King," Reverend Fitzsimmons replied earnestly, missing Alec's humor.

Felicity came sailing into the room,
stopping all conversation cold. Not only was she
wearing her most handsome finery, she had
her hair piled up on top of her head into a
shining pyramid. And crowning the pyramid was the
glittering arch of her mother's heirloom comb.

❧❧❧

Felix referred to his copy of *Secrets of the Occult.*
"According to the ancient seers," he read with glee,
"the end of the world will be foretold by
several unmistakable signs."

⁂

"Felicity stole Great-Great-Grandmama King's comb
then lost it, and she never told anyone about it.
And now she's worried that the end of the world
will come and she'll toast on the Devil's pitchfork,"
exclaimed Felix with delight.

☙☙☙

"Mother, I have to tell you something."
Felicity hesitated, swallowed hard, then,
all in a rush, spilled the rest of it.
"I borrowed your comb and then lost it. I'm so sorry.
I know how much it meant to you and Father."

Conscious of having intruded upon the minister's private moment, Alec got to his feet.

"Well, I'm sorry I surprised you like that," he apologized yet again.

As Alec started to head out, Fitzsimmons scrambled to detain him. There was never a wrong time to chastise one of his flock.

"Mr. King, I'm afraid you distracted the congregation somewhat on Sunday."

Alec immediately looked so guilty that the minister felt compelled to soften the reproof.

"No! No! When a congregation does not listen, it is the capability of the preacher which falls in doubt." He paused, remembering his training. "We were taught that the voice is the preacher's most valuable tool. It's another reason I started flying kites. I would send them up as far as I could and then preach to them, you know, learn to control my voice and make it strong."

"Did you find, sir, that when you preached very loudly, the kites flew any higher?" Alec couldn't refrain from asking.

A quizzical, surprised expression flew into the minister's face, as though he had never thought of this before.

"No," he had to admit.

Point made, Alec took back his flask, nodded

amicably and headed back into the woods.

Reverend Fitzsimmons, given something new to mull over, watched Alec vanish. Then he turned to where the kite had disappeared into the sky. Perhaps the fleeing Archangel Gabriel, fed up with being shouted at, was giving him an even stronger hint about his preaching.

Chapter Eight

Hetty's dismissive comments to Sara's question about the end of the world had done nothing to resolve the issue in the young people's minds. When Sara's three cousins came over to visit, they sat around in the parlor, struggling with the problem. Felicity, as might be expected, was extremely agitated.

"I don't believe in all this end of the world nonsense," she said fiercely—so fiercely that it was clear the person she was trying to convince was herself.

Felix had been lying in wait for just such a statement. He whipped out the magazine he now carried with him everywhere.

"According to the ancient seers," he read with glee, "the end of the world will be foretold by several unmistakable signs."

"Who cares what that trashy magazine says?" Felicity flung back crossly.

"Fine ... then I guess you won't want to hear the signs." Felix nonchalantly folded up the magazine again and waited for curiosity to get the better of his audience. Young Cecily fell for the bait right away.

"Tell us them, Felix," she begged, her eyes quite round with anticipation.

Felicity, though she said nothing, let slip such a look of mingled dread and fascination that Felix fairly gloated as he thumbed to the dog-eared page.

"'The very earth shall tremble with great force, killing the multitudes and reducing to embers a great city by the sea.'"

Sara suddenly sat up straight. She hadn't expected to take anything Felix said seriously, but she could not ignore the facts.

"San Francisco ... the earthquake," she broke in, referring to that recent and sensational event. The earthquake had started a great many fires, reducing blocks of San Francisco to burnt-out rubble. Of course, many other blocks of the city remained in perfectly good condition, but Sara didn't think of that.

"Those predictions are always so vague ..." Felicity dismissed the evidence of the earthquake with a wave of her hand.

"So would you rather know the signs of the approaching Ice Age?" Felix inquired, quite willing to substitute one disaster for another.

"No, Felix. Put your stupid magazine away. Sara, what did *you* find out about Doomsday?"

With the help of some obscure, very dusty tomes of theology from the very back of Hetty's library, Sara had formed her own rather unique interpretation of the event.

"Apparently, it will be something like the weighing of sugar at Lawson's general store—substituting good deeds for the sugar and sins for the lead weights."

Felicity let out a relieved breath. Judgment based on personal merit was something she understood and something she felt well equipped to face.

"Well then, in that case I should do very well," she announced virtuously. "Currently, the loss of the comb is the only black mark in the ledger of my soul, easily outweighed by my good deeds."

"Don't forget you're ruining your parents' marriage," Felix contributed, in case she had forgotten the ruckus at the church. No way was he going to let his sister think the loss of the comb a mere minor peccadillo.

"Not to mention," Sara added grimly, "how

Aunt Hetty and Aunt Olivia will react when they find out Great-Great-Grandmama's comb is gone."

Felicity winced, scarcely daring to imagine the ire of those two self-appointed guardians of the glorious King heritage.

"I *must* find that comb. Felix, where were we when I started squeezing your head?"

Felicity's anxiety prodded all the children into a renewed search. There was nothing for it but to troop over to the scene of the crime again and start poking around. Felix obligingly pointed out the spot on the barn floor where Felicity had run him to ground and taken him prisoner. Felicity plunged into the hunt, kicking up hay ever more distractedly and pulling apart every musty corner she could find. Felix made a few token gestures to help, all the while tremendously enjoying his sister's fruitless efforts.

As time passed and no comb turned up, Felicity became increasingly frantic.

When every bunch of straw on the barn floor had been turned over, every calf pail looked into and every feed bin searched, Sara and Felicity turned to the next possibility. Perhaps the comb could be replaced so that the adults would be none the wiser. To this end, Felix, Felicity and Sara scurried straight over to Lawson's general store to see what they could find.

Needless to say, heirloom combs, especially large, mother-of-pearl ones with a hundred years of history to them, were not often offered for sale at Lawson's. Sara and Felicity examined every comb Elvira Lawson had to offer, only to find them all skimpy, plain and distressingly modern.

"None of these will do," sighed Felicity in weary disappointment.

Scanning the inadequate selection, Sara had to agree.

"Hardly. I think you're just going to have to tell them the truth."

Mulling over this fearsome possibility, the girls started to walk out. But they were only halfway to the door when they overheard Mrs. Lawson talking to one of her customers, a farmer who had come in for some flour and a pound of nails.

"It gave me quite a start," the fellow was saying, "whatever it was."

"I can imagine," answered Mrs. Lawson. "An angel?"

The girls froze in their tracks, especially when the farmer nodded. He seemed inexplicably composed for a man who had just sighted such a radiant heavenly visitor.

"With a trumpet," he told the storekeeper. "Passed right over the silo."

As if angels appeared over Avonlea every other day, Mrs. Lawson continued with wrapping up the man's order in brown paper.

"Must be that Reverend Fitzsimmons," she commented, as though the minister were personally responsible for attracting angels specifically to plague Avonlea.

"Not your run-of-the-mill preacher," the farmer agreed, gathering up his purchases under his arm.

Felicity, quite white about the lips, was staring at Sara.

"Did you hear that?" she whispered fearfully.

As if this weren't enough, Mrs. Rachel Lynde marched into the store next, puffed up with even more astounding news. Mrs. Lynde was a woman of strong personality. When she spoke, there was no choice but for everyone to listen.

"I wouldn't have believed it if I hadn't seen it for myself. Elvira, camomile soap and a packet of washing tablets."

"Why don't you tell that one to the paper?" said the farmer beside her. He, apparently, already knew what Mrs. Lynde was talking about.

Mrs. Lawson stopped halfway to the shelf where the washing tablets lay.

"What happened?"

Rachel Lynde needed no prompting. She leaned

halfway over the store counter, her eyes bright with the pleasure of passing on news of a scandal.

"At the Carstairs's funeral, right in the middle of the eulogy, Henry sat straight up in his casket, looked all around at the candles and said, 'Whose birthday is it anyway?'"

"You don't say," gasped Mrs. Lawson, much more impressed by this story than by the sighting of an angel.

Felicity was by now stiff as a poker inside her dress. First angels—and then the raising of the dead! Terrible things seemed in store for Avonlea.

"Felicity, I'm sure there's a perfectly logical explanation," Sara tried to reassure her, not at all liking the queer shade Felicity was turning.

Once the gossip mill at Lawson's store got going, it was hard to stop. It produced yet more prodigies. Felicity couldn't have been moved by a team of mules.

"Just the other day," the farmer contributed, "old man Steele's cow gave birth to a two-headed calf."

Elvira Lawson's fingers flew to her lips, but Rachel took it calmly.

"I heard about that," she said, obviously thinking a two-headed calf was not a patch on her story about the resurrected Henry Carstairs.

Felicity was now the color of whey in a churn.

"The signs," she rasped. "Felix, where's your magazine?"

Felix had Felicity right where he wanted her. He whipped the magazine from his pocket and waved it at her.

"See, it's true!" he gloated. "Better find that comb fast, Felicity, or you'll be roasting in the eternal flames."

With the sound of the sulphurous fires crackling around her ears, Felicity backed right into the store newspaper stand.

"Felicity, are you all right?" inquired Mrs. Lawson, suddenly noticing Felicity's shakiness.

"You look," added Mrs. Lynde, with a very unfortunate turn of phrase, "like it's the end of the world."

Before anyone could start mentioning talking gateposts or showers of bullfrogs raining from the sky, Sara began to push her cousins towards the door.

Felix, determined to wring out every drop of melodrama that he could, dug in his heels. In the silence could be heard the clop of hooves, no doubt from some farm horse plodding down the street.

"Felicity, don't go out there," Felix gibbered. "You can't go out there."

"Why not?"

"It's them!" Felix made his eyes as big as dollar pieces and knocked his knees conspicuously together.

"Who?" Felicity asked faintly.

"The four horsemen of the Apocalypse."

Felicity's nerve broke. With a cry, she bolted clear out of the store and fled down the street in a total panic, leaving the door banging behind her.

Sara turned furiously on her young cousin. "Felix, this is not funny. What we need is to bring her to her senses or find that comb."

"That's no fun at all," Felix chirped heartlessly.

"Felix!"

"Oh, all right. But how?"

Sara knew only one person who could deal with mysteries ordinary people couldn't unravel on their own.

"Who found you when you were lost in the woods, and who figured out why the Kinghams' well went dry?" Sara prodded.

"Peg Bowen."

Sara nodded emphatically. With Felix in tow, she set out to collect Felicity from whatever corner she was cowering in. Then they would all pay a visit to the Witch of Avonlea.

Chapter Nine

Peg Bowen lived by herself in a cabin deep in the woods around Avonlea. The cabin could be reached only by a narrow, winding footpath, which few of Avonlea's citizens were brave enough to dare. Peg was a stubborn free spirit who did what she liked and said what she liked and hadn't the least interest in living the way staid Avonlea people thought a female should live. Consequently, grown-ups often chased her away when they saw her, and children whispered to each other that Peg could turn them into barn cats whenever she chose!

Sara and her cousins, however, had discovered that Peg was a source of wisdom beyond anything their own families could provide. Her help with obstinate problems no one else could solve was downright magical! When Felix had practically forgotten his alphabet, Peg gave him a special pebble that helped him win the biggest spelling bee the Avonlea school had ever been in. When Edward Ray and Peter Craig were close to death from a fever, Peg's brew of healing herbs had saved them. When the children were trying to get bashful Jasper Dale to propose to their Aunt Olivia, Peg's love potion had nearly caused Felix to end up engaged to *two* future wives! Naturally,

Peg seemed the obvious person to consult to get the hard facts about the end of the world.

Sara, Felix and Felicity hurried down the path to Peg's cabin, where Peg boiled up her concoctions in a large iron pot over a wood fire. Peg's pet raven blinked her yellow eyes and croaked at the children's approach. Several cats, who might once have been inquiring children themselves, moved lazily aside when the young people skittered to a halt.

Peg wasn't surprised to see them. She was never surprised to see anybody. It was as if she always knew ahead of time who was going to turn up on her doorstep.

The cousins ended up seated in a row inside the cabin, sniffing warily at the queer-smelling tea Peg had just served them in big, clumsy mugs. Despite their friendship with Peg, the children could never be quite comfortable with her. Peg always remained mysterious, unpredictable and just a little bit scary. There was no way to tell exactly what she might do or say next.

The inside of Peg's cabin was crammed to the rafters with inexplicable oddments and hung everywhere with the bunches of herbs and leaves that Peg used in her brews. A stuffed monkey, with a little too much mold on its fur to be inviting, reflected the firelight eerily in its staring glass eyes. Lining the windows to keep out the cold were moth-eaten old blankets that swelled with every gust of wind, just as though the cabin walls were breathing under the smoky shadows flickering from the fire. And glowering down at the children from high atop a heap of musty books sat a real human skull!

"Now," asked Peg, sipping the dark stuff from her own beaten-up mug, "what has the finding of this comb to do with the end of the world?"

Under a thatch of wild gray hair, Peg had shrewd, twinkling eyes and a weathered face that nobody could put an age to. Her clothing consisted of incongruous layers of whatever would keep her warm—men's or women's, Peg didn't have the slightest care. Her stout boots, scarred from tramping about the countryside, stuck out from under the fraying hems of her skirt and were planted firmly on the floor in front of her visitors.

Felix, who had gotten over his terror of Peg after she plucked him from a deadly snowstorm and kept him warm in her cabin until he was found, was only too delighted to explain.

"Felicity stole Great-Great-Grandmama King's comb then lost it, and she never told anyone about it. And now she's worried that the end of the world will come and she'll toast on the Devil's pitchfork."

This was accurately put and far too uncomfortably blunt for Felicity. Not only that, Felix wriggled his eyebrows as he spoke and cast meaningful glances at the mysterious and macabre human skull.

"Shut up, Felix!" Felicity growled, looking slightly ill.

Something like a flash of humor appeared in Peg's eyes. She made a show of thinking the matter over.

"I don't suppose," she mused, "the girlie has considered just telling her mother the truth and facing the consequences of her foolishness?"

"That's what I suggested, too!" Sara informed Peg. She still couldn't understand why Felicity didn't take the obvious step.

Felicity sighed, a woman caught in the toils of a dilemma. "I wanted to," she confessed, "but there was never the right moment. Couldn't you just help find the comb? You found Jane Spry's lost cat last month."

If Felicity could only find the comb herself, she could face the end of the world with a clean conscience, and escape all the uproar at home, besides.

"The comb doesn't meow outside my door in the middle of the night," Peg commented coolly. "And the whole point of the end of the world is that it takes you by surprise."

The logic of this statement couldn't be avoided. If the Archangel Gabriel provided advance warning, people would selfishly repent in droves. There'd hardly be a sinner left to make the ambush worth all the trumpeting.

"But there have been so many signs!" Felix insisted, determined to keep up the pressure on Felicity. "Earthquake, fire, a typhoon in India."

"Those are signs, all right," remarked Peg with a wink. Signs of nature in a bad mood and of human carelessness with matches.

As three sets of eyes remained fixed steadfastly upon her, Peg could see that the children were not going to be satisfied with mere talk. They had come expecting magic and would not leave satisfied until they had it. She jumped to her feet suddenly and pulled out a dented silver tray. The metal gleamed darkly through its ancient tarnish. Mysterious burn marks dotted its scalloped rim. Why, it might once have belonged to a tribe of gypsies or a magician from Cleopatra's Egypt, it looked so old.

The children watched breathlessly as Peg opened a small leather bag and shook a pile of reddish powder onto the tray. As she did so, Peg closed her eyes and rocked on her heels, communing, the children were convinced, with unseen forces that would help her with the task ahead.

"The truth is," Peg began, drawing herself up imposingly and lowering her voice, "that every so often, the measure of the world is taken. So far, there has always been more virtue than evil. More good people than bad. But if that balance ever changes ..."

"Doomsday!" supplied Felix, now not so sure whether he was joking or not, for Peg had that effect on people. Felix failed to notice that Peg was simply subscribing to Sara's bag-of-sugar theory, only putting it into more dramatic terms.

Peg nodded gravely. "Even so! The thing to do is admit your weaknesses and failings before the world ends."

Peg paused to let this sink well in. Then she looked at each of the children in turn, as though their failings and weaknesses were written on their faces for her to read.

"I'm going to be wanting your solemn vow that whatever you discover here today in this room goes no further."

Such a promise was only to be expected when magic was involved. With Peg's brow deeply furrowed and her expression so stern, the children were impressed with the seriousness of the matter.

"I don't have to rub spit on my heart, do I?" Felix inquired, remembering the last time he had been forced to take a vow.

Peg curled her lip. "Disgusting, that. No, a simple promise will do, lad. Do I have your word?"

All of them promised earnestly, crossing their hearts and hoping to die. Satisfied, Peg flourished her hands in the air, mumbled a string of strange words and touched the powder on the platter with a candle flame. Instantly, it exploded with a tremendous bang. A billow of colored smoke boiled into the children's faces, temporarily obscuring everything.

Rooted in their seats, the children watched, terrified, as Peg emerged from the smoke transformed. Her eyes rolled back in her head, her hair stood out in spikes, and her arms waved in the air. As though in the grip of some kind of trance, she wailed in horrible tones even as she lit a second pile of the exploding powder. As it went off, she screeched at the top of her lungs. Felix clutched Sara and Felicity sank her fingers into both of them in terror. It was obvious Peg was receiving knowledge that was almost too dreadful for a mere human being to bear.

"Tomorrow night," Peg moaned, swaying, "the voracious wolf will run across the sky! And if the balance of evil in the world is more than the balance of good, the moon will be swallowed by the ravening wolf."

"Sure," Felix chattered through his teeth, "but it doesn't say anything about that in my magazine."

As if the mere mention of something as trivial as a magazine were an insult, Peg shrieked even louder and flapped her arms like windmill sails. She looked so frightening now that the children lost their nerve altogether and bolted, flying out of the cabin and racing down the path through the woods as though the ravening wolf were already at their heels.

Behind them, Peg Bowen fell into giggles as she flung open window after window to let out the smoke from her cabin.

"In other words," Peg chuckled gleefully to herself, "a lunar eclipse." Oh what a wonderful joke. She hadn't had such an entertaining time in months. And she was dead certain that the missing comb would be confessed to before tomorrow night.

The children fled very far down the track indeed before they finally stopped running and crumpled against the trunks of trees, gasping from their flight.

"What are we going to do?" Sara quavered, so filled with alarm by Peg's performance that she now believed in the end of the world almost as much as Felicity.

Felix, who until now had thought he was just using a magazine to scare his sister, was in much the same condition. A whole new possibility opened horrifically before him. What if the magazine article were actually true?

"You think the world really will end tomorrow night?" he asked, his eyes very big and his bravado completely gone.

"We should go to the church," panted Felicity, ignoring her brother and trying to think of the safest place possible. Surely the Archangel Gabriel would think twice before blasting the very cradle of Avonlea Presbyterianism!

"We won't see a thing from the church!" Felix objected.

"I mean," retorted Felicity, "to pray."

Even the impending end of the world was not enough to interest Felix in praying. If the world was going to be laid waste by a ravening wolf, he wanted to at least see it from the best vantage point.

"We should all go to the top of the barn," he urged.

"The lighthouse!" Sara exclaimed in a burst of inspiration. "It's stood up to hurricanes and lightning!"

Felix was in instant agreement, wondering why he hadn't thought of it himself. The lighthouse was a high tower that looked out over land in one direction and sea on the other. There was no way the Archangel Gabriel or the ravening wolf would get by them there.

"We'll get a good view from there."

"And Gus is away working in Markdale," Sara remembered.

Young Gus Pike, the children's very good friend, lived in the lighthouse when he wasn't off picking up jobs where he could to support himself. Gus wouldn't mind in the least if the children used his quarters as a viewing post.

"Drat!" Felicity sputtered, coming round yet again to the source of her troubles. "I wish I could find the comb!"

If she could just find the comb, the single blot on her record would be wiped out. Avonlea would then be so resplendent with virtue that the Archangel Gabriel would surely see there was no point in even stopping there.

"I wish we could warn the others." Sara sighed, taking a wider view. It really was a shame to have to keep such earth-shaking knowledge all to themselves when all the sinners in Avonlea could be given a head start in cleaning up their records.

Felicity looked shocked. "No way! We made a solemn vow!" She wasn't, at this late date, going to add oath-breaking to her baggage of dark deeds.

"We're agreed, then?" Felix persisted, getting to the practical stuff. "We'll meet at the lighthouse tomorrow night." He was recovering from his experience at Peg's and beginning to be quite interested in the wolf.

They all nodded. Sara hurried off towards Rose Cottage and something comforting to eat. Felicity, followed by Felix, turned towards King Farm. Doggedly, she planned to keep up her search for the comb until the last possible minute.

Chapter Ten

In the King farmhouse, Janet was continuing her surreptitious search for the missing comb. She was now so desperate that she was tearing the cushions from the couch in the bedroom, peering beneath the bed, shaking pillows and turning out the contents of the drawers she had already checked a half dozen times before. She was beginning to look nearly as crazed as Felicity.

Alec, unnoticed in all this flurry, was walking by with an armful of kindling for the fireplace. Glancing through the bedroom door, he caught Janet down on her hands and knees thrusting her arm as far as it would go under the heavy maple dresser.

Drawers stood open all around, the doors of the wardrobe were gaping, and even the chest where the summer quilts were kept had its contents spewed out on the bed. Puzzled, Alec stopped and stood for a few moments, watching his wife's antics.

"You lose something?" he was finally driven to ask.

Janet jumped as though Alec had fired a gun behind her, and she nearly cracked her skull on the dresser above her head.

"Alec King, are you trying to give me apoplexy?" she snapped.

Alec looked nonplussed. He wasn't used to being so surprising in his own house.

"I've got to start wearing a cow bell," he said. "I must be the most frightening man in the county!"

Luckily, Alec had too much kindling in his arms to pursue the matter further. He continued on down the hall towards the fireplace.

Once he was out of sight, Janet released the breath she had been holding and resumed her wild search. But when her greatest efforts failed to produce the comb, she had no choice but to give up. Very worried, she put the room back to rights and tried to get on with her day. She knew it was only a matter of time before her husband got back to the subject of the missing heirloom.

She was perfectly right, though this time, Alec at least waited until after the children were in bed. He and Janet had retired to their own bedroom, and Janet was just congratulating herself for having gotten through a whole evening without a word about the comb when Alec started up.

"Do you remember that dreadful pipe your father gave me as a wedding present?" Alec asked her, working on a stubborn collar button.

"Of course I do," Janet said, little suspecting where this conversation was headed. "You fouled the air with it for six months."

"Exactly—and you know why? Because I wanted to keep peace in the family. I didn't want to insult your family. And so I went out of my way to please your father—which was not easy. The comb was given to you as a sincere gesture. And Hetty and Olivia will be hurt if you don't wear it."

In the bedroom next door, the one shared by Cecily and Felicity, Felicity had been lying under the covers, staring at the ceiling, deeply troubled—a state only to be expected in someone with private knowledge about the nearness of the Last Trump. As soon as she heard what her father was saying, she sat up, clutching her pillow, more distressed than ever.

"I am aware of my obligation to your family,

Alec," she heard her mother say defensively, "and I will fulfil it."

"When?"

"Oh, I don't know. I have to find the right moment. Oh Alec, don't try to blackmail me."

Children hate to hear their parents quarreling at any time, but it is doubly troubling when the Archangel Gabriel is about to thrust himself rudely into the midst of their disagreements. Felicity slid out of bed and tiptoed out into the hallway, listening tensely to her parents. Cecily padded up behind her, followed in a minute by Felix.

"They don't know it's their last night on Earth," Felix whispered.

"What else would you call it?" Janet complained to Alec from behind the bedroom door.

"Where," muttered Alec, "there's a ..."

Felicity was unable to bear another word. Spurred by Felix's observation, she rushed into her parents' room, startling them both mightily.

"Stop!" she pleaded. "It's only a *thing*. Surely what is best in our family has nothing to do with *things*."

Alec and Janet looked at each other, slightly amused, but also touched. Felicity was not in the habit of bursting through closed doors.

"Look," Felicity rushed on, "I certainly love

you both, and the baby and Cecily and even Felix ... despite all the material things that I have been denied."

If this wasn't exactly the most tactful way to put things, Felicity more than made up for it by hugging her parents so vehemently that they both had to pry themselves free.

Naturally, Janet supposed all this commotion was about the comb. Determined to reassure her obviously agitated daughter, she made a reckless pledge.

"Well all right, I'll wear it," she promised. "The new pulpit arrives tomorrow. I'll wear it at the ceremony."

"Thank you." Alec was delighted that the matter was resolved—and that he had won. "I'll see to it our loving children get back to bed."

It was a good thing Alec didn't look too closely at Felicity's face just then. The promise Felicity's mother had just sprung on her was about the last thing she had had in mind when she dashed into her parents' room. Now matters were, if possible, worse than before. Oh, if only the arrival of the new pulpit weren't scheduled, so very inconveniently, to arrive before the end of the world!

"Good night, Mother," Felicity mumbled, making her escape before anything else could go wrong.

As Alec led Felicity off, Janet realized what she had just committed herself to and fell back on the couch, completely flummoxed as to what she was going to do. She could not appear again without the comb and survive the King family outrage.

"I'm sorry," she muttered, "that the Yankees didn't burn Fort George to the ground!"

Janet had the whole night to think about her problem and, by morning, she had resolved upon a desperate course of action. As the family gathered at breakfast, she informed them that she was going to Carmody as soon as the breakfast dishes were washed. Carmody was bigger than Avonlea and offered a number of services not to be found at Lawson's general store.

Alec frowned. "Why a trip to Carmody? What's there that I can't pick up for you in Avonlea?"

"I don't want to burden you with detail," Janet replied evasively. "It's woman's business."

"Oh, I see." Alec was suitably put down. "Will you be back in time for the new pulpit?"

"With time to spare."

"I think I might finish cleaning the carpets and some of those other household chores you've been struggling with this week," Felicity volunteered, very anxious to take advantage of having the house to herself. She was feeding baby Daniel at the breakfast table while Felix busily devoured a large helping of eggs.

Quickly, Felix stifled a snicker, while Janet looked at her daughter in surprise. This was much more work than even conscientious Felicity was accustomed to taking on without parental prodding.

"What's come over you?" Janet asked. "This house has been turned upside down."

"She's *combing* it from top to bottom," snickered Felix wickedly.

As Felicity stared daggers at her brother, Alec beamed at his daughter's burst of industry.

"She found the watch fob I'd lost, oh, eight years ago," he mentioned approvingly.

Instantly, Janet pricked up her ears. "Have you come across anything else of interest?" she inquired, baldly fishing for news of any recently discovered combs.

Felicity sighed gloomily and shifted the baby in her lap. "No."

Disappointed, Janet sighed. "Well obviously, it's nowhere in this house," she murmured before she realized what she was saying.

"What isn't?" Alec asked.

"Why, anything Felicity hasn't found, of course," Janet put in, quickly covering her gaffe.

Felix knew exactly what everyone was talking about. Enjoying himself tremendously, he couldn't resist one more dig at his beleaguered sister.

"She's cleaning the place like the Devil's after her."

His reward was a treacherous kick under the table. Even though the plates rattled and Felix barely smothered an outraged squawk, Janet and Alec were too preoccupied to notice.

Taking the buggy, Janet hightailed it to Carmody just as fast as she could go. Her business took her straight to the jeweler's, where it soon became very clear why she didn't want her husband along. She waited in suspense while the jeweler, with his jeweler's glass screwed firmly into one eye, bent over the daguerreotype of Great-Grandmama in New York. What he was looking at was the prominent crest atop Great-Grandmama's head—the famous King family comb.

"Well, can you do it?" Janet asked anxiously.

The jeweler was a rather wizened man with a face permanently stiff from the weightiness of his craft. He sucked in his lips, stroked his chin and finally nodded.

"Certainly."

Janet felt her knees go quite weak with relief.

"It has to look so much like the original that no one can tell the difference." If the Kings ever discovered that the comb was a duplicate, Janet might as well pack up and leave the province.

The jeweler stroked his chin again, but found himself up to even this challenge.

"This afternoon," he confirmed ponderously.

"Thank you."

The thanks were deeply heartfelt—until Janet found the jeweler regarding her steadily with unblinking eyes. At once, she took some money out of her purse and plunked it down on the counter.

The jeweler looked from Janet to the money and back again. His eyes still didn't blink, and one of his brows rose slowly up in silent comment upon the sum offered. An heirloom comb to be created in a single afternoon was no small favor to demand of a put-upon craftsman.

With a sigh, Janet relinquished the rest of the bills in her handbag, then escaped before the jeweler could demand her eyeteeth, too.

Chapter Eleven

Over at the Avonlea Presbyterian Church, the doors were flung wide and a wagon was backed up to the church steps. The new pulpit was finally being delivered.

Reverend Fitzsimmons stood eagerly watching as Hank Webster and a helper wrestled the item off the back of the vehicle, over the church threshold and up the aisle. The old pulpit, which had so recently come to grief under the minister's thumping fists, was set aside. The gleaming new one, exuding the intoxicating smell of sanded wood and freshly dried varnish, was set carefully in its place. It looked strong enough to withstand a dozen ranting ministers and a lightning bolt besides.

"Beautiful! Wonderful!" the minister cried admiringly. His eyes shone at the thought of all the wonderful sermons he could preach from behind such a handsome piece of carpentry.

"Sturdy maritime oak," Hank told the minister proudly. He gave the pulpit a rap with his knuckles to prove how sturdy it really was.

The proximity of the pulpit was too much for Reverend Fitzsimmons. Unable to stop himself, he stepped up behind it, sucked in an enormous breath and burst spontaneously into a chorus from *The Messiah*. Hank Webster flinched as the sound soared to the rafters and back again. There was no denying that, if a listener's eardrums could take it, Reverend Fitzsimmons certainly could sing.

Clad in his churchgoing suit, Alec was pacing up and down the front hall of the house, listening to the clock tick the minutes away. The dedication ceremony for the new pulpit was about to begin, and Janet was, as usual, not yet ready. The buggy was waiting, and even the horse seemed anxious to get the church to inspect the new acquisition.

"Janet! We'll be late!" he yelled up the stairs, wondering why on earth his wife could never be on time.

"Yes, Alec, I'm coming! Coming!"

Janet hurried down followed by Felicity, who was carrying the baby. Felicity was looking from one to the other of her parents, as if she might never see them again.

"Maybe you should take the Bible with you tonight," Felicity suggested with great concern.

"The family Bible?" Alec asked, astonished. "Why?"

"Just in case."

"In case of what?" Janet inquired as she hastily pulled on her coat and gave her hair a last pat in the hall mirror.

Felicity hesitated, then could contain herself no longer. The dread event might happen right in the midst of the church service.

"The end of the world?"

Alec's jaw twitched, but he was in too much of a hurry to reply. Nevertheless, as he hurried Janet out the door and shut it behind him, he couldn't help looking back over his shoulder.

"Sometimes I worry about those children."

Their behavior had seemed very strange recently, between Felicity's insatiable desire to do housework and the way Alec had found every forkful of hay in the barn turned upside down.

Janet didn't bother to answer. She seemed too preoccupied with her own thoughts, which, from the tiny smile on her face, seemed agreeable ones. In fact, the whole atmosphere around her had changed since her return from Carmody. A great weight appeared to have lifted from her shoulders. She headed for the buggy looking quite smugly pleased with herself.

Wondering if his wife was even listening, Alec glanced at her. And, naturally, he noticed her unadorned hair.

"Janet, what about the comb?" he exclaimed, hitting upon the one subject guaranteed to get through to her. His sisters would be at the service. He couldn't show up again unless the famous family heirloom showed up, too.

Janet refused to be unsettled. She allowed Alec to help her into the buggy and arranged her skirts around her on the high buggy seat.

"Alec King, I told you I would wear it and wear it I will."

The moment Alec and Janet went out the door, the children rushed to get ready for their own expedition. Tonight was the night they were going to the lighthouse to witness the end of the world. Felicity had been left in charge of Daniel, so she went upstairs to bundle up the baby for the trip. When she returned to the kitchen, followed by Cecily and Digger, she found Felix with an open gunnysack, loading it with every edible he could lay his hands upon.

"What do you think you're doing?" Felicity cried, seeing all the cupboard doors standing open.

Without missing a beat, Felix stuffed half a meat pie and a great handful of home-baked cookies into the sack.

"If it's the end of the world—no use in being hungry," he told his sister. And since there'd be no use for food after the grand event, Felix intended to eat up as much beforehand as humanly possible.

Inside the church, the pews were already filling up for the dedication service. Hetty and Olivia, punctual as usual, brushed past Rachel Lynde on their way to the King pew. As Rachel turned, Hetty's sharp eyes spied a puff of white sticking out of Rachel's sleeve.

"What's that in your hand, Rachel?" Hetty asked. "Cotton?"

"Yes it is," Rachel replied, a trifle shortly, even as she stuffed the rest of the cotton batting up out of sight.

"Whatever for?"

Rachel gripped the organ music more tightly under her arm.

"Well, I seem to have a bit of an earache, that's what. Not that it's none of your business, Hetty King."

Rachel wasn't about to confess that it was intended to block out the preaching. As the organist, poor Rachel had to be closer than anyone to the minister's bellowing. Rebuffed, Hetty and Olivia moved on to take their seats.

"If he yells at us again tonight," Olivia murmured, "we're going to wish we had some of that cotton."

As soon as Alec arrived at the church, Hetty jerked her chin towards him to alert Olivia. As they both waited for Janet to follow, the light of battle flashed in Hetty's eye.

"She'd better be wearing that comb," Hetty muttered. "It's a slight against our family, that's what it is."

Alec joined his sisters and sat down quietly. They waited with the rest of the congregation as Rachel began to play the organ. Music was customary before the service to cover the sound of people settling themselves and to get them into the proper pious mood, though piety seemed to be the last thing on Hetty's and Olivia's minds.

"Alec, should I go and check on Janet?" Olivia inquired rather pointedly as the moments slid past. "She's taking ages."

The artificial cherries atop Hetty's brimmed hat quivered with indignation. "Oh now she's afraid to face us, is she?"

"Now Hetty ..." Alec began placatingly, "she's just taking a minute to fix her hair after that windy buggy ride." Alec was praying that Janet, for goodness' sake, was going to show up wearing the comb.

A sudden, astonished buzz of conversation behind them made them all turn. Janet was walking up the aisle towards them. She was wearing the comb. And, despite the nods and frozen smiles she managed for her neighbors, she seemed to be actually squirming as she walked, caught in the throes of the most excruciating embarrassment.

It was no wonder that the entire congregation was staring in disbelief at the top of Janet's head. Great-Grandmama's comb—or at least the new version of it—stuck its teeth deep into her hair and stood straight up in ostentatious, brazen glitter. Far too large to suit Janet's features, it looked as though it might topple her over if she didn't take care how she stepped. Its color clashed with her hair and, altogether, it appeared the most absolutely hideous *thing* anyone could have wished upon the poor woman, a tiara straight from Hell.

"Good Lord!" Alec squeaked, aghast. No wonder Janet had waited until reaching the church door before sticking that monstrosity on her head.

Head high, neck stiff, face burning from all the stares in the church, Janet took her seat beside him.

"How does it look?" she inquired acidly, hoping they were all satisfied now that she had made such a complete spectacle of herself.

"Oh Janet," Olivia choked out, too shocked to be other than truthful, "it's *awful*."

Tougher and more uncompromising than her sister, Hetty was determined not to be swayed by mere appearances. It was the symbolism that mattered.

"Olivia, may I remind you," she said grandly,

"that it is Great-Grandmama King's comb of courage."

It certainly was—and the courage it represented was clearly the courage it took to wear it. Janet hoped Great-Grandmama could rest easy in her grave now that she had inflicted the grotesque thing on the hapless family of her descendants.

Olivia could not take her eyes off her sister-in-law. "I had no idea ..."

Even Hetty shifted uncomfortably now that she had taken a closer look at the overall effect.

"I do recall it looking somewhat more elegant," she conceded, though still unable to admit the fault was with the comb. "It doesn't sit as I remember on you, Janet."

Janet was just waiting for Hetty to say that Great-Grandmama's comb was too grand for a mere former Ward. But it was Olivia, instead, who leaned over.

"Perhaps you should take it off, Janet," she suggested mercifully.

The niceties of taste completely escaped Alec. He could only remember how his eldest daughter had admired the comb.

"One good thing ..." he offered, "someday you'll be able to pass it on to Felicity."

Even Janet had to smile at that thought.

Family obligation at last fulfilled, she thankfully got to slip the comb into her pocket just as Reverend Fitzsimmons swept to his place behind the new pulpit.

Chapter Twelve

While the congregation was gaping at Janet's comb, the children, who were supposed to be at home quietly amusing themselves, were speeding towards the lighthouse as fast as they could go.

Rose Cottage was closest, so Sara arrived first. She stood on the path at the cliff's edge, stamping her feet for warmth and wishing her cousins would hurry up. Behind her, the white wooden tower of the lighthouse stood out against the dark horizon, its light a beacon to the ships at sea but its loneliness not the least bit inviting to children lingering by themselves in the cold.

Before very long, Felicity appeared, much slowed by having to lug baby Daniel with her. She also had a cardboard envelope tucked under her arm. Cecily, beside her, had Digger on a leash. Bringing up the rear was Felix, dragging his gunnysack full of supplies. As the bizarre little caravan drew to a halt, Felicity peered apprehensively at the sky.

"You can tell it isn't a normal evening, can't you?" she said.

Sara, who had had to run across the shadowy fields all by herself, was more than a little uneasy. Of all the children there, she was the one with the liveliest imagination.

"Yes ... it's so very bright ... mysterious."

"It's a good thing Mr. Potts lit the lighthouse," added Felix. The dark of night made Peg Bowen's prediction loom rather large. Felix was glad of the light shining steadily above him.

Sara hopped on tiptoe to peer in the dark windows of the lighthouse's lower story.

"I wish Gus were home," she murmured. They all would have felt safer, even in the face of the Archangel Gabriel, if stouthearted Gus Pike had been beside them.

Since nobody bothered to lock their homes around Avonlea, the children, accompanied by Digger, opened the door and trooped inside. The only light was that filtering in through the window, making the interior spooky and full of shadows. The children huddled in the midst of Gus's humble abode, wondering what to do next. Sara peered up the narrow stairway that led to the upper regions, where the beacon was.

"Shall we go up to the top?" she asked.

It was very black up there and known to harbor bats. Sara was not very keen to climb up, and neither was anyone else. Felicity backed slightly away from the ladder.

"No, let's wait until it's really happening."

Now that they were in the lighthouse, there was nothing for it but to wait. Felix plunked his sack of food down on the floor and Felicity arranged a makeshift bed for the baby, who was already asleep, atop an old trunk in the corner. After they settled, Felix began rooting through the gunnysack. A minute later he was stuffing date squares into his face as though he meant to finish off every date square left in the province. Digger began to drool, his hopeful gaze following every crumb to Felix's lips. Cecily patted Digger. Sara pulled some photographs from her pocket and began to look them over as best she could in the dim light.

"What did you bring, Sara?" Felicity inquired.

"Some photographs of my parents before they got married."

"That's not very practical," Felix told her. "You can't eat photographs."

Sara's mother had been Ruth King, sister to Alec and Hetty and Olivia. Ruth had died of tuberculosis when Sara was very young. It had taken years for Hetty to forgive Blair Stanley for whisking Ruth away from Avonlea to marry her, even though Blair had provided a life of comfort, wealth and exciting travel for his adored wife.

Still eating, Felix went to the narrow window and opened it. The moon, full and gorgeous, hung in the starry sky.

"What did you bring, Felicity?" Sara asked.

Felicity lifted the envelope she had been clutching to her bosom.

"My report cards. I thought they might stand me in good stead as a sort of record of my achievements."

"What about you, Cecily?" Sara turned to her youngest cousin.

"I brought Digger," Cecily told them simply. "I wouldn't go anywhere without him." Cecily still wasn't quite sure what all the furor was about, but she wanted Digger with her nevertheless. He'd stick by her, no matter how many angels blew trumpets in his ear.

"Just like Felix wouldn't go anywhere without food," Felicity clucked disapprovingly. Typically, Felix seemed to have absolutely no sense of the seriousness of the situation. The end of the world appeared to be some sort of spectator event to him, requiring lots of snacks and a front row seat at the lighthouse. Well, he'd know how serious it was when a big, brawny angel grabbed him by the scruff of the neck and put him on trial for gluttony!

"You'll be glad when it happens and somebody thought to bring lunch," Felix shot back, still munching. Taking care of his stomach really was Felix's number one concern in life.

Without warning, the moon darkened, a huge shadow galloping across its face. Everyone screamed and jumped a mile.

"False alarm!" Felix assured them breathlessly. "It was just a cloud."

The children collapsed against each other. The moon, in its full radiance, returned to light the night sky.

In the Avonlea church, the congregation was bracing itself for the expected roar from Reverend Fitzsimmons. Some were wincing and putting in earplugs. Others gripped the edges of their seats, took deep breaths and gritted their teeth. However, when the good Reverend began, he spoke in a mild voice.

"I was out in the fields, the other day, the beautiful white fields of Avonlea, practicing tonight's sermon, and I was surprised by a man out walking ..."

Here, he looked straight at Alec, who was a little taken aback by this individual attention.

"So surprised, in fact," Fitzsimmons went on, "that I fell backward and struck my head. And it occurred to me then, that if I hadn't been hollering at the heavens like a fool, I wouldn't have been so surprised. And that led me to think that perhaps, sometimes, silence is a better tool for a preacher than bluster. A sin of pride—to place the loudness of my voice above the importance of the message in the words. So, rather than my voice alone, let's raise our voices together in song, and bless this pulpit."

He signaled to a bewildered Rachel Lynde, who had to hastily unstuff her ears and start playing.

Hetty looked at her brother and relaxed her rigid shoulders.

"This fellow may work out after all," she observed, approval generously creeping into her voice in spite of all the possible improprieties the fellow might yet commit.

Chapter Thirteen

In the lighthouse, the children continued with their eerie vigil. After the false alarm they had had, time seemed to drag on interminably.

Felix stood guard at the window, eating steadily to fortify himself and keeping his eye on the moon. Baby Daniel happily slept on, quite oblivious to the approaching disintegration of his small, comfortable world. Increasingly spooked, Felicity seemed barely able to keep herself from gnawing her fingernails and pacing a groove in the floor. Sara hugged her photographs. With the suspense building, they all felt the need to be doing something, but none of them knew what.

"Peg Bowen said we should try to clear our guilty consciences," Sara suggested slowly, unaware that Peg had simply meant that Felicity should confess to her mother the truth about the comb.

"That's right," Felix chimed in. He was feeling a bit queer himself. He hadn't believed in the end of the world one bit until Peg Bowen got involved. Now he was growing less and less sure of himself. Just suppose, he asked himself, it really happened!

Felicity turned righteously to her brother. "My conscience," she assured him, with more conviction than she felt, "is as clear as a pearl."

"What's a conscience?" Cecily asked. She was wondering whether she had one and, if she did, how she would get it clear.

"It's the record of our weaknesses and failings," Sara explained. Her solemn expression seemed to say that, even at their tender ages, the record could be long and black indeed.

All the children thought hard. Felix even wrinkled his nose and chewed his lip with the effort.

"I have something," he announced suddenly. "Felicity, I once used the loving cup that you won for naming the books of the Bible as a tadpole trap."

Felicity was very particular about who touched her things. Indignation flared in her eyes—and was swiftly extinguished.

"Aah. Well, boys will be boys," she managed, bravely expanding the limits of her tolerance.

Cecily, who wanted to get in on the confessionfest, opened her mouth.

"I once—"

"I also used a pair of your bloomers for a flag on the top of our treehouse," Felix broke in, daring to look directly at his sister.

In spite of herself, Felicity flushed dangerously.

"Who saw them?"

"Well, let's see ..." Felix paused thoughtfully and made a slow count. "Everyone."

A picture of Edward Ray and Rupert Gillis and all the rest of Felix's crowd, snickering and hooting while her undergarments flapped on a pole, burned itself into Felicity's imagination.

"I ... forgive you ... Felix," Felicity choked out, barely keeping herself from going for his throat.

Seeing his sister's heroic self-restraint, Felix realized he was safe from retribution—at least on an earthly level. He began to expand inside. He would never get such an exquisite opportunity to torment Felicity again.

"I read your diary," he boasted, now on a roll. A fellow could enjoy even the end of the world if it gave him the pleasure of flaunting all the secret triumphs he would never have dared admit aloud before.

Felicity began to breathe hard and clench her fingers into fists. She didn't trust herself, even under these extreme circumstances, to let Felix live. Felicity's diary was sacrosanct. She kept it hidden in a place where she thought no one would ever find it. She wrote in it every day, pouring out her innermost thoughts. Oh, how *dare* that treacherous little fiend lay a hand on it!

"I think we've had enough confessions," she flung out hastily, attempting to cut off the flow of appalling revelations before things came to blows.

"I read it aloud," Felix persisted, watching his sister gulp in a lungful of cold night air.

"To who?"

"My friends. We were camping out. Everyone laughed at the gushy parts about Gus Pike."

At the mention of Gus, Felicity's face flamed scarlet. A great many of her secret thoughts concerned Gus Pike. Gus had kissed her once, and she'd been melting secretly at the thought ever since. And she would rather have been fried alive in old crankshaft oil than have anybody know.

"Gus Pike!" Sara exclaimed, forgetting her photographs and spinning round to stare at her cousin. So that was why Felicity always stood up so staunchly for the unpolished lad.

"Gus Pike didn't laugh," Felix gloated, unable to resist delivering the final blow. "But his ears burned a fierce red."

Felicity's jaw flapped open, her eyes bugged and the envelope full of exemplary report cards crashed to the floor.

"You read it to Gus Pike?!"

Felicity was unable to imagine anything more calamitous. She began to swell up ferociously. All her muscles tensed for a lunge at her brother.

"Felicity! Don't lose your temper! THE END IS NIGH!"

Sara's shout did nothing to halt Felicity. She looked as though every blood vessel she had was about to pop. The end of the world seemed puny beside Felix's dastardly outrage.

"Hang Doomsday!"

Felicity sprang at Felix. Taken by surprise, he managed to jump clear of her first frenzied sally. But a moment later, he stumbled over one of Gus's fishing rods and she had him in her grip.

Hands around Felix's throat, Felicity backed him up, step by struggling step, until she slammed him up against the windowsill and thrust him halfway out. Upside down, Felix could see nothing but the night sky, scattered stars and the huge white moon. Yet even though a corner of that moon was turning black, no one noticed. Felix and Felicity were locked in mortal combat while Sara jerked madly at the tail of Felicity's coat. If Sara didn't break up this fight, she might be witness to a homicide then and there.

"No, Felicity!" Sara yelled. "It will look very bad for you if you murder Felix!"

"I don't care! He deserves it!"

Felicity jammed Felix farther out of the window. Finally, from his topsy-turvy position, Felix twisted his head back far enough to spy the dark spot on the moon's edge spreading. He went rigid in Felicity's grip, scarcely able to believe what he was seeing.

"The wolf!" he screeched out. "The wolf is here!"

Felicity stopped squeezing her brother's windpipe. Sara and Cecily rushed to the window to gape out.

It was true! A fearful dark arc was cutting into the silvery brightness. The moon was being devoured by the wolf before their very eyes.

Felix dropped weakly back inside the lighthouse as Felicity let go. All the children stood petrified, faces to the sky, their mouths agape.

"Felicity! Don't you want to unburden yourself before the end?" Sara asked in a small, shaky voice. The Archangel Gabriel might rend the heavens with his trumpet any moment, and then all confession would be too late.

"No! I'd rather not."

"I do," Cecily piped up, infected by the terror of her elders.

As more of the moon vanished, Felicity found herself badly torn. She hated to admit she was anything less than perfect, especially in front of her brother. But neither did she want to go to Hell.

The interior of the lighthouse became darker and darker, and the awful stillness was broken only by the ragged breathing of the frightened young people inside. Felicity couldn't take her eyes from the moon. As it was gobbled up, an eternity roasting in flames began to seem a very high price to pay for keeping a few blemishes to herself. Fear finally won out.

"All right, all right!" Felicity blurted. "I ... I ... copied some test answers from Sara once in arithmetic."

"That's the spirit!" Sara encouraged.

"I have something to confess," Cecily tried to say.

Felicity rushed on with her own recitation. Her sins grew even worse.

"I ... have feigned illness on occasion to avoid Sunday services."

Even this shattering revelation failed to stop the ravenous wolf in the sky. The moon was almost completely eaten up by blackness. Only a slim silver shimmer remained. Felicity remembered what had happened to Lot's wife, turned into a pillar of salt merely for peering over her shoulder against orders. By contrast, her own trespasses suddenly loomed into towering crimes. If Lot's wife had been so badly punished for such a small thing, Felicity thought, what must await a wretch who had lost the King heirloom comb and then done everything she could to cover up the infamy?

"Doesn't anyone want to hear what *I've* done?"

Cecily piped up, afraid she wouldn't get her chance before the moon was gone.

She was too late. As Cecily finished speaking, the moon vanished completely. A blackness enveloped the countryside so thick and dense that even a light-house bat wouldn't have dared to venture into it. Certain it was all her fault, Felicity cracked totally.

"I am black-hearted and vain," she wailed. "I stole Mother's comb and then lost it and didn't have the courage to tell anyone about it. Oh, I wish I'd told Mother, and if the world weren't ending I swear I *would* tell her."

Incapable of further speech, Felicity sank against her brother. Shivering, she waited for a divine hand to pluck her bodily from the light-house and cast her to her fiery doom. A horrible silence descended again as the children clung to one another. Finally, Cecily took advantage of the cosmic upheaval to get a word in edgewise.

"Digger took the comb."

The words seemed to quiver in the air above their heads.

"What?!"

Sara's cry rang out just as a tiny sliver of light illuminated the landscape. It was as though Cecily's small voice had been all that was needed to heal the world, though everyone was too startled by what had just been said to notice.

"That's what I wanted to tell you," Cecily said in a small, quavery voice.

"Why didn't you take it away from him?" Felicity had now recovered enough to think of all the trouble she had been put to because Cecily hadn't spoken up.

"He *liked* it. Besides, I thought you'd brain him, like you did Felix."

"Cecily, Digger is a *dog*!"

Light, still unnoticed by the children, now penetrated the interior of the lighthouse and illuminated Cecily's taut little face. Cecily had been hugging Digger tight all the while. She didn't believe that being a dog was sufficient protection from her sister's violence.

"I was just going to let him play with it for a while—but I think he buried it."

"Oh, this is a terrible thing that you've done, Cecily," Felicity exploded. "I'd hate to see what will happen during your Judgment."

Suddenly thinking he might have his own vast load of sins, Felix had hunched his shoulders and gritted his jaw against Gabriel's summons. When nothing seemed to be happening, he dared open one eye to peep at the sky. What he saw was the returning light.

"Look!" he breathed.

All eyes turned to the moon, which was now one-quarter exposed and slowly grew in its brightness. At once, the children started jumping up and down and cheering for joy. Their heroic confessions had stopped the hairy devourer and made him spit out the moon.

"We have turned the balance of evil," they exulted, dancing madly around Gus's simple home.

Cecily beamed, certain it had been her final words that had done the trick. Felicity, acutely aware of her own vast contribution to the effort, now turned a grim eye to Felix.

"You still have *me* to deal with, however."

Grasping at some excuse to escape her, Felix groaned, clutching his midriff.

"Aaagh! My stomach!"

Outside, the moon burst free of the last of the blackness. It hung above, white and plump, no worse at all for its journey through the gullet of the wolf. As for the Archangel Gabriel, he had obviously given up any idea of a sneak attack on Avonlea. For all the children knew, he might very well have flown on all the way around the world to China to console himself with a century or two of misdeed-hunting among the vaster population there.

Chapter Fourteen

Felix managed to survive Felicity's vengeance, mainly by racing to the farmhouse well ahead of her. Sara gathered up her cherished photographs and hurried back to Rose Cottage. Tempted to pursue Felix, Felicity luckily remembered to collect baby Daniel from atop the trunk. Cecily put the leash on Digger, who showed not the slightest remorse at being exposed as the guilty party in the loss of the comb.

All of them managed to get home and slip innocently into their beds before the grown-ups returned from the church. The rest of the night passed without any avenging angels, celestial wolves or any other divinely instigated tormentors.

Not everyone slept peacefully, however. At least two of the residents of King Farm had some time in the small hours to truly examine their consciences.

When the first pink of dawn crept along the horizon, the old Leghorn rooster in the barnyard woke. He crowed energetically just as a sleepy Janet, clad in robe and slippers, groped her way downstairs. Alec was already out in the barn milking the cows and doing the morning chores. When the children came down, everyone would expect a hearty breakfast on the table.

Janet's eyes were still half closed and her hair awry. She arrived in the kitchen yawning hugely. But her yawn snapped shut in surprise when she discovered Felicity already there. Felicity was fully dressed, very nervous and sitting bolt upright in the old wooden armchair. She looked very much like a prisoner steeling herself for a trip to the guillotine.

"Well, you're up early," Janet observed, wondering whether Felicity was bent on polishing more floors and dusting behind more dressers before going to school that day.

Felicity had been up for a very long time, and she had been using the time to think. The more she thought, the more she realized that there was only one thing to do. The events of the previous evening had showed her that she could not get away with keeping her sins to herself, and she was determined to get the worst over with right away.

"Mother, I have to tell you something."

She hesitated, swallowed hard, then, all in a rush, spilled the rest of it.

"I borrowed your comb and then lost it. I'm so sorry. I know how much it meant to you and Father."

Felicity had no idea about the copy of the comb Janet had had the jeweler in Carmody construct. Nor did she know that Janet had worn it to the service and thus managed to satisfy the family honor. Remembering only her mother's rash promise of the day before, Felicity supposed her mother had gone, combless, to church and been mortified before the entire congregation.

Janet stood stock-still in astonishment as she grappled with this piece of information. What a deal of arguing—and what a mountain of house-work—could have been avoided had Felicity only confessed earlier!

"Oh Felicity, you should have known better. After I expressly told you not to."

Felicity hung her head, flushing at her mother's rebuke. She had always been so very proud of her own good sense and exemplary behavior. How humiliating it was to have to openly acknowledge such foolishness.

Seeing Felicity's distress, Janet glided the rest of the way into the kitchen, where the fire, stoked by Alec on his way out to the barn, crack-led lazily inside the stove. She couldn't let her daughter suffer without taking her own share of the guilt.

"But I have something much worse to confess, Felicity," Janet went on, prodded by her own uncomfortably compromised scruples. "I've no right to be angry with you."

Felicity blinked at her mother very hard. "I beg your pardon?"

"Well I thought *I'd* lost it. So I went to Carmody and spent all our mad money on a duplicate. It turns out that if I'd simply put the thing on, Hetty would have understood immediately why I hated it so much." Then, because of all the fuss that had been made, she added with a grin, "I shall surely go to Hell."

Felicity shivered at hearing her mother say such a thing so lightly. She was still weak from having so recently escaped a run-in with the Archangel Gabriel and she hadn't yet regained her sense of humor. Now that she was doing the right thing, she wanted to do it thoroughly.

"I've heard that confessions are good for the soul. Perhaps if we told Father ..."

Janet nearly dropped the piece of firewood she had been getting from the woodbox.

"Oh," she said hastily, "I think it's good enough we told each other, Felicity. Now if the real comb doesn't show up, we're safe."

The two females suddenly smiled at each other with a new understanding—and a new complicity. Let sleeping dogs lie, the proverb went—and let pacified relatives enjoy their happy ignorance.

Janet put more wood in the stove, then opened a

cupboard in order to get breakfast started. She found the cupboard completely bare. Unable to believe the naked state of her previously well-stocked shelves, she turned to Felicity in amazement.

"What's this? Scavengers have stolen all of our food overnight?"

Felicity shrugged, knowing it would not take her mother long to come up with the obvious suspect. Janet marched straight to the bottom of the stairs.

"Felix King!" she hollered. "You get down here this instant! I have some questions for you."

So intent had Felix been on keeping clear of Felicity that he had clean forgotten to bring back the gunnysack from the lighthouse. Now, shrinking, he remembered just how much he had managed to stuff into it. He had better think of a good defense very fast. He ducked deep under the covers.

"I don't feel well," he groaned back, trying to sound as sick and pathetic as he could.

Meanwhile, Digger was busy in the yard. Digger hadn't acquired his name for nothing—digging was one of his favorite occupations. He was digging vigorously now because he had a large bone in his mouth and needed a place to store it.

When he dropped the bone into the fresh hole, it clanked loudly on something beneath it that was certainly not soft earth or another bone. Before Digger could fill in his handiwork again, a pair of farm boots tramped up behind him and a hand reached into the hole. When Digger tried to protest the invasion of his private larder, he found himself pushed away.

"Digger! Get out of there. Go on."

The hand belonged to Alec King—and it had just pulled the original heirloom comb from the dirt.

"What's this?" he sputtered, staring down in utter confusion at the object in his hand. "I must be hallucinating." He wiped away the dirt from the hidden treasure and, sure enough, the winking fake jewels and the unmistakable mother-of-pearl ostentatiousness of Great-Grandmama's comb appeared.

"Well, I'll be!"

Alec scratched his head and turned the comb over in his hand. Surely he had seen his wife wear it to the church only the evening before. What had she done, sneaked out in the dark of night and buried it like some unwanted corpse?

His brows flew together. He turned towards the house and raised his voice.

"Janet?" he called out. "Janet?"

When no answer was forthcoming, he started off towards the kitchen, determined to get to the bottom of the mystery.

Inside, Janet and Felicity saw what he had in his hand and looked rather frantically at each other. But by the time Alec got there, they had collapsed with laughter. If confession was good for the soul, then their souls were about to be benefitted very much indeed. The awful secret simply refused to be kept—or rather, buried. And now the King family was going to have not one, but *two* hideous heirloom combs to plague the next unsuspecting females to inherit them.

Skylark takes you on the...

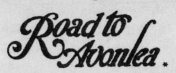

Road to Avonlea *

Based on the Sullivan Films production adapted from the novels of
LUCY MAUD MONTGOMERY

- [ ] **THE JOURNEY BEGINS, Book #1** $3.99/NCR   48027-8
- [ ] **THE STORY GIRL EARNS HER NAME, Book #2** $3.99/NCR   48028-6
- [ ] **SONG OF THE NIGHT, Book #3** $3.99/NCR   48029-4
- [ ] **THE MATERIALIZING OF DUNCAN McTAVISH, Book #4** $3.99/NCR   48030-8
- [ ] **QUARANTINE AT ALEXANDER ABRAHAM'S, Book #5** $3.99/NCR   48031-6
- [ ] **CONVERSATIONS, Book #6** $3.99/NCR   48032-4
- [ ] **AUNT ABIGAIL'S BEAU, Book #7** $3.99/NCR   48033-2
- [ ] **MALCOLM AND THE BABY, Book #8** $3.99/NCR   48034-0
- [ ] **FELICITY'S CHALLENGE, Book #9** $3.99/NCR   48035-9
- [ ] **THE HOPE CHEST OF ARABELLA KING, Book #10** $3.99/NCR   48036-7
- [ ] **NOTHING ENDURES BUT CHANGE, Book #11** $3.99/NCR   48037-5
- [ ] **SARA'S HOMECOMING, Book #12** $3.99/NCR   48038-3
- [ ] **AUNT HETTY'S ORDEAL, Book #13** $3.99/NCR   48039-1
- [ ] **OF CORSETS AND SECRETS AND TRUE, TRUE LOVE, Book #14** $3.99/NCR   48040-5
- [ ] **OLD QUARRELS, OLD LOVE, Book #15** $3.99/NCR   48041-3
- [ ] **FAMILY RIVALRY, #16** $3.99/NCR   48042-1

*ROAD TO AVONLEA is the trademark of Sullivan Films Inc.

TRUTH OR CONSEQUENCES

When Felicity finally reached up to tidy her loosened coiffure, she felt around frantically on top of her head, then froze. Great Great Grandma's comb, so firmly stuck into her topknot, was missing. Panic raced up Felicity's spine.

"It's gone!" she squawked. "Mother's beautiful comb is gone! Find it! We have to find it!"

Without a thought for her dress, Felicity dropped to her knees and started digging around in the hay that surrounded her. Soon she had Sara and Felix out in the barn rooting around in the hay with her.

"It's not here," Sara concluded.

"Look again!" Felicity begged, unable to believe the large, mother-of-pearl inlaid comb could simply disappear.

"Can't you just tell Aunt Janet you're sorry?"

"Sara, it's an heirloom! the gift of that comb means the world to Mother."

Like her Aunt Hetty, reverence for family treasures ran deep. Felicity could not escape the fact that she had broken express orders not to wear the comb and was headed for dire punishment over its loss.

"I bet it's worth a lot of money," Felix added, twisting the screw a little tighter.

At this, Felicity broke down completely. Putting her hands to her face she began sobbing aloud.

Also available in the Road to Avonlea Series from Bantam Skylark books